In Bed with

Anne
Boleyn

In Bed with

Anne Boleyn

A Novel

LACEY BALDWIN SMITH

AMBERLEY

First published 2014

Amberley Publishing
The Hill, Stroud
Gloucestershire, GL5 4EP

www.amberley-books.com

British Library Cataloguing in Publication Data.
A catalogue record for this book is available from the British Library.

ISBN 978 1 4456 3447 0 (paperback)
ISBN 978 1 4456 3455 5 (ebook)

Typeset in 11pt on 12pt Sabon.
Typesetting and Origination by Amberley Publishing.
Printed in the UK.

Contents

Chapter I   York Place   7

Chapter II   Enter the Falcon   29

Chapter III   Sex and Revolution   87

Chapter IV   The War Against the Monks and Friars   131

Chapter V   The Self-Fashioned Man   157

Chapter VI   Killing the Falcon   183

Chapter VII   The Rising Phoenix   239

CHAPTER I

York Place

It was a gorgeous June day in 1523, the kind for which the only adjectives were wondrous and joyous, and every one of Mark Smeaton's fifteen years thanked God, man and the devil for permitting him to stride through the warm sunshine of a Saturday afternoon some five miles inland from the Thames river and Cardinal Wolsey's great house downstream from Westminster Palace. He was headed nowhere in particular, just ambling for the joy of being away from the congested headquarters of the man who, as Lord Chancellor and Cardinal Legate of all England, ruled the realm in the king's name: more than five hundred legal, governmental and financial advisers, domestic and official servants, and hangers-on of every social status, all jammed into a rambling and not overly clean or sanitary structure called His Grace's household and great hall at York Place.

Thankfully, for the moment at least, the world was empty of humanity except for one adolescent boy liberated from the vile smells and crowded conditions of what passed for the pomp and circumstance of worldly power. Nary a peasant at labour, a sheep at grazing or a horse or ox at work could be seen, only an occasional crow gliding through the silent blueness of the sky and a worried rabbit scurrying through the hedgerows; all this beauty and stillness was for Mark's pleasure and benefit alone, and he did what he did best; he sang as he walked through meadow land and wooded glens.

The voice that emerged to praise the perfection of nature and the optimism of youth was as fresh and newly formed as the June day that blessed the countryside. The exquisite pitch of a true alto joined the chorus of song birds, but was oddly and unpredictably mixed with the comical warbling of vocal cords uncertain whether they were sounding the high notes of a child's countertenor or the bass of the fully developed man. Mark found the mix deeply embarrassing and profoundly frustrating as he was forced to listen helplessly as his throat and sound box decided which he was – an adult or a child. On the positive side, his frustration was mitigated by the knowledge that he had been temporarily rusticated from the cardinal's child choir until his voice had settled down, thereby creating time for solitary treks in the country. With luck in a month or so he would join the cardinal's adult singers; in the meantime he could practice on his two favourite instruments – the lute and the virginal, and learn Latin, the trademark of the true gentleman.

Ahead was a stand of beech trees with their grey trunks and polished leaves standing out against the greenery of pastureland as rich and lush as a Brueghel landscape. As Mark approached, he was startled by the neighing of horses, and the image of two grey horses tethered to a beech tree and bedecked in the cardinal's livery. Further investigation revealed two human forms closely entwined, the man with his breeches down around his ankles, the woman, her bodice pulled down and skirt bunched tightly around her stomach, and both in passionate *flagrante delicto*. Mark was a trapped animal avidly watching a human activity that hitherto had been known to him only through lascivious teenage gossip; at the same time he knew that decorum required a hasty and silent retreat from what was clearly a very private act. Yet he stood there watching, his eyes glued to the woman's disappointingly small breasts but marvellously white thighs and hips. They induced thoughts that Mark would only admit in secret.

Before good manners could generate polite actions, the bodies ceased the rhythm of copulation, and a male voice panted out: 'I lay in your lap and was in paradise. Thank God.'

As the female form began to rearrange her clothing, it answered: 'Don't congratulate God, thank me; God had nothing to do with our pleasure.'

'But I thought you were an untrained virgin,' the man said as he pulled up his hose.

'I was,' came the reply, 'but after six years at the French court you get to hear about every detail of the sex act and how to generate the greatest pleasure for both yourself and your partner. I was putting theory into practice, and if I say so myself, I have been the perfect student pupil.'

'Amen to that' was his heartfelt response, then suddenly he looked up and in an amused voice asked, 'Who is this youngster who has been enjoying and rehearsing our love-making?'

Mark turned to flee, dreadfully aware that the codpiece of his thin summer breeches had begun to fill and bulge. Thinking a strong offence was always the best defence, he turned his head and said, 'I hope, good mistress and master, that you were enjoying yourselves.' Unfortunately as he spoke his voice betrayed him and branded him an adolescent. Worse, he suddenly realised that the shapes so frantically dressing themselves were known to him. Had he been an instant quicker he would have realised who they were and held his tongue. They were proper ladies and gentlemen: Anne Boleyn was known to him as one of the ladies of the queen's chambers and her father was treasurer of the king's household, and Henry Percy was a page for Cardinal Wolsey and heir to the earldom of Northumberland, one of the oldest and most powerful titles in the kingdom. Both were far, far beyond and socially above Mark, the fifteen-year-old son of a Flemish carpenter and laundry-woman mother.

Anne's razor tongue was the first to answer her paramour's question. 'I known this puerile and foreign varlet; he is Mark Smeaton, His Eminence's prize musician.' She spoke as if describing the cardinal's prize bull, a mere animal. 'Boy, what are you doing here, and why aren't you back at Wolsey House singing for your betters? I can guess the reason. From your croaking voice you must have been evicted from the children's choir. You're lucky that we in England don't castrate our countertenors to preserve the purity of their tone. From the size of the stones between your legs I would judge their cropping might be a painful loss to you but little loss to maidenhood. Personally I think you deserve gelding as proper punishment for spying on your superiors.' Her eyes were focused on his crotch where mention of castration had further enlarged his instrument, and he could sense himself blushing crimson from the insulting implications of her words.

He was no child; he was fifteen and had the equipment to prove his manhood that stood erect on command. What did she mean by calling him a foreigner? He had been born in Flanders, true, but had lived most of his years in England while she had spent seven years abroad at the courts of the Archduchess of Burgundy and King of France. She was far more foreign than he and was clearly proud of it. And she had called him a varlet because his parents were not clean-fingered gentlefolk and had to work with their hands for a living. Henry Percy might be of ancient heritage and prestige, but Mark knew enough about Anne Boleyn to know that her great-grandfather had made his money in the wool trade and he and his offspring had used the family fortune to wed their way into the nobility. Hadn't the great cardinal himself started life as the son of an Ipswich butcher and cattle dealer; what might a young man with the voice of an angel become?

Insulted and embarrassed, and close to panic, there was nothing left but to flee. Had he been a dog his tail would have been tucked tightly beneath his belly. The well-bred but flat-chested Anne Boleyn with her sharp tongue and vicious social snobbery must have thought him a cowardly canine, but every instinct told him to turn and run. With Anne's derisive laughter still ringing in his ears he kept to the byways and tilled fields for fear of meeting up on the main road with the haughty Anne and her scrawny lover who had looked so idiotic with his breeches about his ankles and his white ass shining in the sunlight. He was quite certain he could have given this Boleyn woman a far better ride than the overbred Percy. Intense hatred tainted by lust filled his soul, and as he fled he repeated in his mind words that would be remembered for years: 'The bitch, the bitch, the goggle-eyed whore.' Anne Boleyn's insufferable snobbery and wicked tongue had won herself an enemy for life, but he admitted she possessed incredible sex appeal.

As he jogged homeward he experienced a new and exciting sensation, the epiphany of rebirth. With each step the indignity of insult and humiliation receded, replaced by the conviction that the world was his oyster to do with as he pleased, and that revenge and reprisal were his for the taking. By the time he reached York Place he felt transformed, as if a new persona had entered his body. Without warning he knew himself to be a man. He emitted a few musical notes to test their pitch and timbre and was pleased that his voice no longer betrayed him. He could almost feel himself grow a couple of inches in height and develop muscles hidden under puppy fat. Adultness had burst upon him and he even began to think of training for the joust; a singing knight; he burst out laughing in pure pleasure at the thought. How was he to explain such an unexpected and gratifying transmogrification? Was it like the experience of the saints he read about? Had the spirit of God possessed his soul and transformed him? He laughed again; unlikely, he thought, since he had enjoyed too avidly the sight of Anne Boleyn heaving in sexual ecstasy, and he felt no forgiveness to the bitch for having humiliated him without remorse. Revenge was far sweeter than the absolution of the inexcusable. The work of the devil was more likely.

Back at the beech copse Anne and Henry Percy were mounting their horses and debating their awkward encounter with Mark Smeaton. Anne thought the episode comic relief, and laughed at Mark's swelling codpiece and brilliant blushes. Percy was less amused. 'Cock's passion,' he exclaimed. 'If the cardinal hears of this we are both in deep trouble. My father has plans to marry me off to Mary Talbot, the heiress to the Shrewsbury earldom, thereby consolidating his power in the northern shires. She is penis-proof and belongs in a nunnery.'

'All the greater reason for us to get married and thwart such a dreadful fate,' was Anne's amused response, and she leaned over and gave him a satisfying full-mouth kiss on the lips. 'Any chance that the future can be rearranged and the chilly Mary Talbot dispatched by a carefully administered dose of foxglove and monkshood?'

Anne spoke in jest, but Percy looked at her as if she had turned into a witch and sprouted devil wings, and muttered, 'What if young Mark reports our dalliance to the cardinal?'

'He wouldn't dare! If he did I would turn him back into a countertenor,' Anne answered. 'When shall I see you next? I doubt whether my father will again be coming to Wolsey's residence to discuss the king's personal finances with the cardinal, let alone bring me with him. That means you will have to accompany His Eminence when he comes to court to visit the queen, which he does regularly. I am always available though there is little privacy for such pleasures as we have had this afternoon.'

As Henry Percy rode his gelding towards York Place, Anne on her mare caught up with him at a canter, grabbed the gelding's harness and slowed both animals down to a walk. 'You realise,' she said, 'we are pawns in our fathers' schemes for family aggrandisement. We are both being bartered and are at stud, you to the Talbot shrew and me to James Butler. You must know him; he is one of the cardinal's student pages like yourself except that his father, Pier Butler, calls him a prisoner and hostage, not a student, kept by the cardinal to insure his parent's good behaviour in Ireland. My grandfather married Margaret Butler, daughter of the Irish Earl of Ormond. The earl died without direct male heir and my father covets the title. But so does Pier Butler on the Irish side of the family; he is a first cousin once removed to my grandmother. My uncle, the Duke of Norfolk, when he was Lord Lieutenant of Ireland, proposed a marriage between James and me: Pier gets the earldom for life and our first male child get it thereafter. On paper everybody, except possibly James and me, are delighted by the arrangement, and that is why I was hauled back from Paris to satisfy the family ambitions. The only hitch is that neither the king nor Wolsey are enthusiastic, and on second thoughts my father has begun to realise that he would have to wait for Pier to die in order to inherit the earldom. Wolsey thinks that keeping young James as a page and hostage for his father's good behaviour in the bloody anarchy of Irish tribal politics is a better way of controlling the Butler clan than marriage. Why the king is ill disposed, I do not know, but for the moment further negotiations are either on hold or in abeyance. Father hasn't bothered to tell me which.' She failed to mention that she was willing to do almost anything to avoid marriage into the Butler family with its dreary Irish castles and barbaric tribal retainers.

The passage of time can be as elastic as a musical rubato, for some stretching out into an eternity, for others as brief as a lightning flash. Two years had crept by with the noiseless footsteps of daily routine. Mark Smeaton was now seventeen going on a quarter century, fully developed in mind and body, fair of hair, handsome of face and spectacular of body, waiting impatiently for what fortune's wheel might have in store for him. He was now not only one of the cardinal's sixteen singing men but also His Eminence's favourite songster who could perform in three languages – English, Dutch and French. At the moment he was sitting on a bench in one of the anterooms to Wolsey's bedchamber, waiting for His Eminence to change his clothes and rest from an exhausting day at Greenwich Palace where he had waited upon the king and attended his council.

Sitting next to him was George Cavendish, a pedantic but friendly little man who was never seen without quill and paper in hand to document every event and thought of the cardinal's daily routine. He was one of twelve gentlemen ushers and served the cardinal as if he were the living Christ, a monument to flawlessness, whose every word was divine. Even Mark regarded him as overly naive and ridiculously ardent in his devotion to a cardinal whom Mark thought should never be underestimated despite his overweening pomposity. Two generations of Cavendishes labouring in the royal exchequer collecting what the king was owed in taxes and fees had bred the perfect bureaucrat, always anticipating the cardinal's every wish and whimsy.

Cavendish had adopted Mark as a surrogate child for his own children were back in Glemsford, Suffolk, where his wife lived for most of the year without a husband. He supervised Mark's schooling, corrected his Latin grammar and educated him in the intricacies of the cardinal's household, a beehive of the strictest custom based on degree, priority and place, and a crowded garden of weeds thriving on acrimony and the rivalry of too many servitors for too few jobs. Mark often thought that the nursery rhyme of the helpless king who asked for a bit of butter for his royal slice of bread and discovered that it took an eternity to find someone low enough in the pecking order to oblige him was a perfect picture of Wolsey's domestic reality. Every man had a job, no matter how trivial or servile, to which he clung as tenaciously as a mollusc to a ship's hull for fear of being ignored, or worse, superannuated. A multitude was forever clamouring at the cardinal's door willing to fulfil the most menial job. There were always two candidates for Wolsey's personal cupbearer, carver, server and waiters, in all some forty people to attend upon his table and fetch him dinner.

Every position, from the master chef dressed in damask, satin and velvet and a gold chain around his neck, to the gentlemen ushers of the bedchamber, had yeomen, grooms and serving boys beneath them. The kitchen of the great hall possessed a myriad of offices:

two cooks, two clerks, a comptroller, a surveyor of the dresser to oversee the serving of food, a clerk of the spicery, a yeoman of the scullery with a legion of children and women to do the scrubbing, and many more officers for the larder, scalding house, buttery, pantry, ewery, wine cellar and stables. Every servant had a coveted role to be performed exactly as tradition slavishly prescribed it. George Cavendish could describe every function of the household from the principal offices of steward, treasurer and comptroller down to the lowest scullery urchins in the kitchen, the day labourers rowing the cardinal's barge and the varlets cleaning out his stables. Cavendish himself regulated the daily ritual of the household, supervising the rhythm of the dining hall, catering to the banquets and masques required to entertain important guests and ambassadors and organising the elaborate masquerades when the king came to visit his invaluable and marvellously efficient chief minister, who thought nothing of entertaining and feeding two hundred guests at a single sitting. When the king arrived in disguise the cardinal indulged him in the elaborate travesty of pretending not to recognise the six-foot two-inch giant figure of his royal master.

From the windows of the anteroom where Mark and his mentor sat overlooking the river, they could see the cardinal's private and ornate dock and barge bedecked with the crimson livery of his cardinalate colours. Wolsey was a confirmed ritualist insistent that political power and social position must always be properly garbed in the visual and musical symbols of authority. Almost every event, from the daily ordeal of eating dinner in the great hall to travelling upstream a few hundred yards to the king's Palace of Westminster that housed Parliament and the law courts, was accompanied by the pomp of ceremony and the sound of music, be it the beat of drum, the quaver of the lute or the blast of the trumpet. When the ranking cleric of the kingdom rowed down the Thames river headed for the city of London and Greenwich Palace it was Wolsey's God-ordained due that Londoners should doff their caps in respect for divine authority.

His Eminence never appeared in public without the Great Seal of England displayed in front of him and his cardinal's hat resting on a cushion carried by a high-ranking nobleman. Two silver crosses, two pillars of silver and a sergeant-at-arms bearing a mace of silver gilt preceded his arrival while his twelve gentlemen ushers shouted out, 'My lords and masters make way for my lord's grace.' His entire entourage was dressed in cloaks of scarlet trimmed in black velvet, and in his hand he bore a hollowed-out orange filled with vinegar and spices to curb the noxious street smells on his way.

His sense of importance knew no bounds and he was acutely aware of the historic rivalry between the archdiocese of York and Canterbury. Centuries before, the Archbishop of York had claimed precedence over Canterbury by usurping the arch-episcopal throne and Canterbury had felt obliged to reinstate his authority by literally sitting in his lap. When in 1513 Wolsey was appointed Archbishop of York he revived the ancient struggle and as soon as he became cardinal legate demanded and received a position in front of and superior to Canterbury. This is why he was always preceded by two silver crosses carried by two of the tallest and comeliest priests in the kingdom to emphasise his superiority to Canterbury which had rights only to one cross, and he urged his royal master to present him with the office of Lord Chancellor which had previously belonged to William Warham, Archbishop of Canterbury. Precedence, recognised and acclaimed by all, was an essential attribute of power, while ritualistic repetition gave meaning and stature to every action no matter how trivial. His Grace never went to bed, no matter how exhausted, without completing to perfection his divine prayers, and he was forever berating the forty-six yeomen who daily attended his person, laid out his clothes, made his bed and did his bidding. It was an axiom of daily life that those in power must never be victimised by their servants.

Oddly enough Mark and Cavendish were chatting about a similar domestic problem: how to discover and keep singers with trained voices satisfied with their pay, board and keep, and how to keep peace between the cardinal's sixteen secular singing men and twelve ecclesiastical singing priests, not to mention the constant importation of talented but difficult foreign singers and musicians who expected special treatment and praise. The competition between hall and chapel was blatant and often poisonous. For Mark the distinction was nothing more than two kinds of music – secular and ecclesiastical. Anything more was the result of clashing artistic temperaments that he found repugnant and incomprehensible. His own disposition seemed quite different. He delighted in the joust, craved above all else to be accepted as a gentleman, and – his mind refused at first to give words to his thought – he longed to teach mistress Anne Boleyn humility and repentance for the sins of yesteryear. He had not forgotten or forgiven her description of him as a puerile, foreign varlet with worthless testicles.

As they spoke Thomas Cromwell, one of the cardinal's chief lawyers and a Member of Parliament, entered the antechamber asking whether His Eminence had arisen. He wanted to know the cardinal's plans for reforming the Church and dissolving a few of the smaller monasteries, the wealth to be used to endow new educational institutions at Ipswich, the cardinal's birthplace, and Oxford. As he listened, Mark made a bet with himself that at least one of the new colleges would be named after the cardinal to assure his future renown. When advised that his master was not available, Cromwell made it clear he was prepared to stay and converse, and asked whether they had heard that Henry Percy and Anne Boleyn had been seeing one another so often and so intimately when Wolsey and his pages visited the queen's chambers that they were now officially engaged and were planning their marriage. 'The word is all over the queen's chambers.'

'I can't image what she sees in him other than a prize title,' Mark quipped. 'Other than a name he has nothing to recommend him, certainly not his scraggly, scrofulous posterior. He is a three-inch folly. Does His Grace know of these developments? It is not as if their affair was anything new. It's been going on for at least two years.'

'Even the king knows,' Cromwell laughed, 'and is not pleased. He doesn't approve of attractive young damsels leaving his court for marriage and the pleasures of Christian intimacy approved by the Church. I wonder whether it is tied up with his frumpy and overly pious wife and his own envious and wandering eye. To answer your question: no, our master the cardinal does not know, at least not as of this morning.'

'You are probably right,' Mark agreed. 'Years ago the king made it impossible for Anne Boleyn to marry young James Butler when he was a page in the cardinal's household and actually forced the cardinal to send him back to his father in Ireland unwed. You know, of course, that the king has been looking at Anne's sister, Mary Boleyn, with wolfish eyes and asking about her reputation at the French court where her incontinence was much appreciated, it is said, even by the French king. Henry obviously wants to have the Boleyn girls close at hand.'

Mark liked the burly Thomas Cromwell with his round face, piercing eyes and mop of unruly hair. He sensed a kindred spirit, a self-made man and son of an ironmonger and brewer, who knew the value of a well-placed bribe and was as scornful but secretively envious of aristocratic posturing as any child of a Flemish carpenter.

At that moment the door to the cardinal's private closet banged open and out stamped the great man, obviously not in a tranquil temper. 'I have just received orders from the king. Get me Henry Percy, NOW,' he bellowed. 'Why can't that Boleyn girl keep her French ways and enticing smiles to herself and quit corrupting my pages. Percy knows full well that anyone of his rank never marries without first receiving the king's consent. Not to mention his father's blessings.' In a few minutes Mark was vastly entertained by the sight of a scared-looking Percy being hauled by the ear off to a public scolding in the long gallery where Wolsey could exercise by walking back and forth the length of the room and indulge his anger by berating the hapless Percy. The entire household gathered to watch the performance.

The cardinal's first words set the tone of the drama. 'I marvel not a little of your peevish folly, that you would tangle with a foolish girl in the queen's chambers. I speak, of course, of that floosy, Anne Boleyn. She is nowhere near good enough for you. I speak of both her social rank and moral character. Anyone brought up in the French court will have acquired the worst characteristic of a bawdy house. You don't seem to realise that you will soon inherit from your father one of the worthiest earldoms of this realm, and you should have asked the consent of both your father and the king. Are you blind to the estate that God hath called unto you? You have engaged yourself to be married without regard for the public consequences that belong to the king, and the family consequences that belong to your father. Had you discussed the matter with either of us we would have found you a wife suitable to your estate and honour. Had you done so you would have stood high in the king's estimation.

'But now behold what you have done through your wilfulness. You have offended not only your natural father but also your most gracious sovereign lord, and matched yourself with a common trollop who is nothing more than a fortune hunter. She wants to be Countess of Northumberland. I have little choice but to inform your father, who will break your ill-advised marriage contract or disinherit you.'

During this tirade Percy was squirming with rebellion, almost in tears in his determination to defend his actions and Anne's reputation. 'Sir,' he cried out. 'I knew nothing of the king's interest in my love life and I am deeply sorry I have earned his displeasure. But I am of age and must make my own decisions in life. I have sufficient means to support any wife who takes my fancy, and though she be a simple maid and her father is only a knight, she is nevertheless descended from the highest noble parentage. Her mother is sister to the Duke of Norfolk and her father a linear descendant of the Earl of Ormond. Why should I then, Sir, be hesitant to wed the young lady whose estate is equivalent with mine when I come into my inheritance? Therefore it seems to me instead of upbraiding me you should be entreating the king to grant his princely benevolence and support what is now my public engagement to Mistress Boleyn. Both my conscience and my honour are at stake.'

Wolsey could hardly believe what he was hearing: arrogant rebellion, not humble submission. His face became the colour of his crimson gown. 'Boy,' he bellowed, 'you have no choice in this matter. You can't possibly believe that your conscience outweighs the king's pleasure or that a king and a cardinal cannot allay the prickliest conscience.'

Faced with the inevitable, Percy collapsed. No one, he thought, could be expected to withstand the fury of this irate cleric. 'Forsooth, my lord cardinal, if it pleases Your Grace, I will submit myself wholly to the king's majesty in this matter, my conscience being discharged of the weighty burden of my precontract with Anne.'

'Excellent,' Wolsey breathed more easily and his complexion returned to its normal pale pink. 'I will send for your father and together we will find the means to disembarrass you of your hasty folly.'

If Percy thought that his father, who as fifth Earl of Northumberland bore the same name as his eldest son – Henry Algernon – would be any less intransigent or outraged than the cardinal he was sadly mistaken; young Percy's utter defeat and humiliation was in the making. Upon the earl's arrival at York Place his words brooked no argument. 'Son,' he said, 'you have always been a proud, presumptuous, disdainful, and a very unthrifty waster as your present actions confirm. What joy, what comfort, what pleasure can I conceive in you who thus without discretion or thought misuses yourself, having no regard for your father, for your sovereign to whom all loyal subjects owe faithful and humble obedience, or for your own estate which you have endangered by your engagement to this Boleyn wench. Your lightness of head and wilfulness has earned you the displeasure of the king, which is intolerable for any subject to sustain. Worse, the king's displeasure and indignation has cast me and all my posterity into utter ruin and desolation. Mercifully, our king is a kindly and forgiving prince, and the lord cardinal has devised a way for me to unravel your unholy mess. I pray God that your redemption will be a sufficient admonition and warning to be more careful and intelligent in the future. If you do not mend your prodigality I foresee you destroying all that I have devised. Thankfully, I have other sons, and I will not hesitate to disinherit you should you fail to reform yourself.'

During this diatribe the earl had been pacing up and down the long gallery crowded with the enthralled and listening retainers of the cardinal. He now turned to the crowded room and said, 'Now, masters and good gentlemen it may be your chance hereafter when I am dead to see the proof of my predictions should my son continue his dangerous ways. In the meantime, I ask you all to be his friends and tell him his faults when he acts foolishly. That is the sign of true friendship.' He then took his leave of his son and bid him 'go your way and attend upon my lord's grace your master and see that you do your duty. I should caution you that as soon as I return to my estates I will make possible your marriage to Mistress Mary Talbot, who will make you an appropriate wife.'

After long debate and many letters, Percy's engagement to Anne Boleyn was dissolved and his marriage to the Talbot heiress arranged. Anne was greatly offended by both, and Wolsey saw to it that the Boleyn filly was removed from the queen's service and sent back in disgrace to her father's home at Hever Castle in county Kent. The cardinal's household returned to relative peace and quiet disturbed only by the memory of the cardinal's high-handed and unnecessary public handling of the Percy crisis and the debate over whether young Percy and his would-be bride had received a grievous injustice.

Mark Smeaton thought the cardinal had earned himself yet another bitter enemy, which was dangerous and politically unsound, but he rejoiced at the harsh and tactless words directed at both victims, whom he thoroughly detested. George Cavendish never thought to question the rightness of his master's decision; Thomas Cromwell wisely kept his thoughts to himself.

CHAPTER II

Enter the Falcon

Henry was seated nude on the edge of his bed; he liked the contrasting sensation of naked vulnerability and regal omnipotence. Moreover, he vastly admired his splendid body that at the age of thirty-two still embodied all the finest attributes of royalty – voluptuous and vigorous. He watched languidly while Mary Boleyn dressed herself; an attractive sight but one without lust or reverence. He felt no love for the blonde and shapely body before him, only the fading memory of a joyous ten minutes in bed. All he said was 'Tell your sister Anne her exile is ended and she is welcome back at court in her old position as one of the queen's maids of honour.' He gave thought to the contrast between the two sisters; so different but from the same nest. He wondered whether there had been a wandering and unacknowledged father. Odd, he thought, that the picture of one sibling should conjure up the image of the other. Mary with her fair hair, Nordic heritage and healthy pink skin was the embodiment of traditional beauty but strangely bland and uninteresting. Anne in contrast with her elongated neck, flat, undeveloped breasts and swarthy dark skin was interesting to study but no great beauty to behold. It was her eyes that held your attention, deep pools sparkling with laughter and amusement and highlighted and enriched by eyelashes and brows delineated in ebony. Those eyes were without rival, alluring, beckoning and filled with promise. Suddenly he quit his musing and spoke; 'Tell Anne to come to court in time for the banquet and masque in honour of the French delegation that accompanied Wolsey back from France.'

The lady holding the king's imagination prisoner was at this moment in a foul mood, complementing the miserable wet fog and drizzle of a late spring day that had forgotten that summer was next on the agenda. Anne was bored to death in her rusticated condition at Hever Castle, exiled by order of a fat and interfering cardinal. Anne had returned to England in 1521 from her seven educational years on the continent with marvellous expectations; she would bewitch a bevy of dashing and rich young studs into passionate courtly love with her French ways, blood-red lips and voice made enticing by its carefully accented Gallic rhythm. From the start she had been a sensation with her heavily French-accented English at the masque and banquet given in honour of the Imperial ambassador who had crossed the channel to negotiate a possible marriage alliance with the six-year-old princess Mary Tudor.

The theme of the festivities had been the cruelty of unrequited love, the setting Cardinal Wolsey's magnificent riverside mansion at York Place. The staging consisted of a spectacular mock attack on a three-towered castle covered with green tinfoil, besieged by eight knights consumed with courtly love, each representing the chivalric ideals of Nobility, Gentleness, Amorousness and Loyalty with Henry VIII leading the gorgeously attired and masked band of heroes. In this Green Castle huddled eight court ladies depicting the finest qualities of the female personality: Beauty, Honour, Perseverance, Kindness, Constancy, Bounty, Mercy and Pity. Anne performed the part of Perseverance, a quality she so admired that it became the hallmark of her career. The attackers hurled dates, oranges and confectionary fruits while the maidens in their fortress returned fire with sweetmeats and rosewater. Maidenhood and feminine beauty were soon overcome and taken prisoners by the king and his jolly followers and escorted off to an elaborate dance and costly banquet where they all unmasked and revealed their true characters.

The essence of courtly love as it had come down from past centuries and become part of court etiquette and performance was love of dressing up in disguise, play-acting to win an audience, and secrecy – secret beauty hidden behind a mask, secret poetry written for a secret lover, secret affairs consummated with beautiful ladies; it mattered little whether they were married or not. At twenty-one Anne was a marvellously graceful dancer, could conceal her identity by disguising her voice and mimicking other accents, and could perform to perfection all the theatrics associated with courtly love. It was in the midst of this atmosphere of make-believe that a bond between England's most Thespian monarch and the daughter of an ambitious knight blessed with unprecedented sex appeal was in the making.

Five years had passed since her triumph at York Place and the Green Castle, and that was in large measure the nub of the problem. Here she was a captive in Hever Castle surrounded by wardens ranging from her father, her mother and aunt and the castle guards with no excitement and nothing to do except read the Bible in French, a pastime that made her feel slightly guilty since English Church law prohibited reading Scriptures in English but said nothing about reading them in French. In the midst of these dreary thoughts Anne heard loud voices at the castle gate. Normally the castle porter would see to the commotion but any distraction was worth her attention if only to curb the ennui, and Anne rose to see who was clamouring at her door.

There at the drawbridge stood Thomas Wyatt, horse bridle in hand and looking as fresh and succulent as Adonis in the company of Venus. His beard was the envy of the court, dark, heavy, and pointed, almost pectoral in length. His eyes sparkled and laughed and his face wore a satirical grin. By his side sat a large grey shaggy dog, most probably of the spaniel engender, with a satirical grin on its friendly mug almost as comical as its master's. 'Anne,' he cried out, 'You are more gorgeous than ever and dressed fit to welcome a king.'

Anne's response was not as cordial. 'Are you planning to bring that beast into the castle? I haven't laid eyes on you for months. Come in.' The dog heard the command 'Come in,' and bolted into the great hall where it turned on Anne, placed its feet on her shoulders and started to lick her face with all the passion of a deprived lover.

Anne screamed; Wyatt shouted, 'Down Gabriel. I apologise for his unacceptable behaviour.' Gabriel obeyed reluctantly and Anne stood there sputtering her fury for all canines.

'Look what that creature has done. It has covered my bodice and blouse with paw marks and turned my face into a Gorgon.' As Anne claimed stage centre, Gabriel investigated the great hall and broke into joyous barking, hurling himself at the far end of the hall, knocking over stools and benches. 'He has found Jane Parker's prize cat,' Anne announced. 'I hope he kills the disgusting thing. He will save my doing so.'

Wyatt interrupted to say: 'You don't seem to have any great love for dogs either.'

She laughed and answered, 'You might add the human animal also.'

'I hope that I am the exception,' Wyatt inserted.

'Possibly; we shall see. Do you know Jane and her feline, Thomas? She has been living at Hever ever since she married my brother George. I don't know what went wrong on their wedding night but ever since they have rarely spoken and George arranges to be away months at a time. She compensates by engrossing herself in alchemy, the occult and working spells. But back to you. This is your first visit to Hever despite the fact that we are distant neighbours. What brings you today to my parental prison guarded by my mother, father, aunt and castle guards? You have no idea what delight it is for me to see a new face ever since that hateful Wolsey exiled me from court.'

'I have often thought about riding the twenty or so miles to Hever,' Wyatt answered, 'but this time your reputation at court was so enticing I decided to investigate the rumours that the exciting Anne Boleyn might be in residence. I also needed a break from married life and nagging children.'

Anne was her usual glamorous self, and promptly suggested that he write her a poem to commemorate their meeting at Hever. Thomas looked embarrassed and began to pace up and down in agitation. 'I can't manufacture poetry on request. I need time to meditate and compose.'

'Of course you can. You are the kingdom's greatest bard and have an unrivalled reputation as Eros. Be creative,' she ordered.

'If you command,' he sighed. 'How about a stanza about your heraldic badge, the falcon:

'Lux! My fair falcon, and thy fellows all;
How well pleasant it were your liberty!
Ye not forsake me that fair might you fall.
But they that sometime liked my company,
Like lice away from dead bodies they crawl:
Lo! What a proof in light adversity!
But ye, my bird, I swear by all your bells,
Ye be my friends, and very few else.'

With a laughing face, Anne exclaimed in carefully staged confusion, 'Your poetry is as convoluted and muddled as ever, Thomas, and I don't like the idea of lice crawling away from a dead body, but I love my falcon jangling with bells so long as we are something more than friends.' He was amused and embarrassed by her reactions. 'I guess,' he confessed, 'I am a gentleman after all. I can usually lie like a trooper but not to you. I didn't compose that poem on the spur of the moment. I spotted a falcon while riding through the forests between our houses, and composed as I rode here. I had just dotted the final 'I' as I arrived. Thus the pleased and grinning expression on my face.'

Anne seized his hand and said, 'Thomas, your dog is still barking though the cat has long since vanished. Put your canine outdoors and we can go upstairs to get away from his noisy sounds of disapproval.' She led him up an impressive staircase to the bedrooms above the grand hall. The room she selected housed a magnificent four-poster bed with a bedspread beautifully embroidered with the Boleyn-Norfolk coat of arms displaying a host of bull's heads and fleur-de-lys. 'This is my parents' bedroom but they are away for several days and their bed is by far the most comfortable.' They sat on the bed and Thomas began to delicately untie the ties holding her bodice and shirt to her skirt.

'This is my favourite part of seduction, the undressing,' Wyatt whispered into her ear. Sexual progress was suddenly interrupted by loud stamping sounds overhead. Anne rose, put back on her skirt, and mounted the adjacent stairs to investigate the sounds. Thomas, semi-naked in bed, decided to await her return. He suffered an hour of erotic imagery of what was yet to come while Anne trotted up the stairs to the chamber above where she found her sister-in-law, Jane Parker, now Lady George Boleyn. 'What on earth are you doing in this shuttered and darkened room, Jane? Your stamping interrupted me in a most intimate encounter with Thomas Wyatt.'

Jane was dressed in a flowing black gown with a veil over her head. From beneath the veil her voice sounded strangely disembodied: 'I apologise, Anne, but the moment has come and I cannot wait. You asked me to cast a spell on Cardinal Wolsey and I have been working on it ever since. The moon and Saturn have to be in the right position and the planets all in a line. Only today, and not again for over a year, will the heavens be in such a favourable alignment.'

'Jane, you have caught me at the worst possible time. Wyatt is undressing as we speak. It was months ago I spoke of the cardinal, and I thought you had forgotten.'

'Well I hadn't. I don't care if his rod is as vertical as the minute and hour hands on a dial clock standing erect at high noon. I have been coordinating things ever since my marriage and I moved into Hever Palace. It has given me something to do other than not perform my wifely duties with a husband who arranges never to be at home. I have everything all ready for the casting.'

'I don't see the "double, double toil and trouble, fire burn, and cauldron bubble," let alone the eye of newt or blinded cat,' Anne said with a laugh.

'Anne, all that is witchcraft and mostly nonsense. I work in alchemy and magic, not with dead bodies, disinterred corpses and mummies.'

'Thank God for that.'

'I have drawn a circle on the floor with the two lines running from its centre thereby dividing the circle into three equal parts. It is a magic circle drawn with a miraculous sword with a charcoal tip to mark the circle. Inside the ring is an inner circle where we will sit around the brazier, which I will light. The three divisions are for the three natural powers or spirits that are willing to do my bidding; Leviathan, Behemoth and Ziz. Like God, no one may speak to the devil directly, you must have a negotiator. Mephistopheles and Beelzebub are too august for the likes of me, so I must do with lesser demons. Leviathan is symbolised by a whale and represents the power of water, Behemoth is a mighty land animal, and Ziz is a giant griffin-like bird, the symbol of all creatures that can fly. Each has its own spell written in Arabic letters in the three sections of the magic circle. I will recite the spells for each power while you drink of thaumaturgic potent I have concocted from ancient alchemical formulas.'

'Are you sure this will work?' asked Anne, suddenly more serious.

'Absolutely, but with Wolsey it may take time. I recall you wanted him to die alone, stripped of all power and fame, and in great pain. That you shall have. Any further requests?'

'No, except you might put in a good word for me with the king. He has been debauching my sister Mary while I am exiled here at Hever. That doesn't seem fair to me.'

'We shall see. Come drink the potent, hold this candle and sit beside me within the inner circle.'

Within minutes, Anne began to feel the strange effects of the liquid and suddenly began to see growling beasts with grinning teeth and saliva-dripping fangs circling the magic circle where they sat. Naked men could be seen dancing in the background, and the metal brazier around which they huddled in the centre of the circle let off great billows of perfumed scent. The fire flamed upward towards the ceiling, the beasts unable to withstand the sudden light receded and the naked men vanished; only Jane's voice reciting the Arabic incantation remained. Finally this also softened and finally ceased. All was deadly quiet; what Anne could only describe as a violent stillness, as if the earth had ceased to rotate and was waiting impatiently to be told to start up again.

Jane rose from her crouching position next to the brazier, went to the windows and threw open the shutters. 'It is done,' she said. 'Nothing left to do except to go back to Thomas Wyatt and put the poor man out of his misery. Not many lovers can say they called up the devil before tupping their paramours.'

'What happened here has put me totally out of mind for sex. Poor Thomas will simply have to wait.'

'Glad to hear it. Come give me a kiss to seal our secrets.' Jane clasped Anne around the neck and gave her an encompassing hug and kiss that surprised and discomforted Mistress Boleyn.

When Anne finally returned to her parents' bedroom, she was as cold and distant as if Wyatt had been sleeping surrounded by week-old dead fish, and he was promptly invited to leave. 'Please go,' she said.

'May I return?'

'Yes, whenever you please, but give me a few days.'

When they met again, Anne favoured starting again where they had left off, but Wyatt was curious about the stamping sounds and Anne's hour-long absence. 'What possessed you,' he inquired, 'Did you have an impatient and neglected lover overhead?'

'That is no kind of question to ask a lady,' Anne's voice was laden with scorn.

'Then why were you gone an hour?'

'I had a meeting.'

'With whom?'

'I was supping with a she-devil.'

'You mean I lay alone in a cold bed while you ate dinner. Well, I hope you had a long-handled spoon while dining with the devil.'

'Of course, I did. Shall we proceed now where we left off last week?'

'By all means!' Thomas Wyatt's hands itched to start their downward descent towards the focus of the miracle of birth and the brink of bliss. Just as he was about to enter the gates of erotic passion his mind unexpectedly offered up a verse from the past, composed for some long-forgotten damsel:

When her loose gown from her shoulders did fall,
And she me caught in her arms long and small
Therewithal sweetly did me kiss,
And softly said, 'Dear heart, how like you this?'

There could be only one answer. In liquid rapture he quenched his flaming desire.

As their arms, legs and lips unclenched and panting breasts relaxed, he murmured, 'That was heaven. We must visit Venus's boudoir again soon? Anne, a question: that reddish spot on your buttock, is it a rash?

'No, it is a birthmark. I can't really see it but my mother always referred to it as Anne's rose.'

Wyatt looked more closely. 'Yes, a rose, perhaps a Tudor Rose.'

'If it is, it is on the wrong sibling; my sister Mary commands the king's bed.' Anne began to dress, and as she bent to pull up her stockings, Wyatt leaned over and slipped her gold necklace with a garnet pendulant into his cupped hand. 'I shall keep this as a precious memento of our love. When shall we meet?'

Anne's answer was sadly abrupt: 'Not till we are both back in Greenwich Palace. I have been ordered back to court. I recently received a letter from my sister who says it is the king's command. The necklace is only a trinket. Keep it for all I care.'

'Oh,' was Thomas's flat reply. Then after a long pause he added as he was leaving: 'I wonder what inspired His Majesty's command? Lust? Politics? Or the desire to surround himself with ladies who are his intellectual equal.'

§

Henry, King of England, stood in one of the bays of Greenwich Palace overlooking the Thames. He looked and dressed every bit a regal prince. His clothes did justice to his status. They magnified His Majesty with shoulder padding to enhance an already impressive chest and forearms, and gems and jewellery to blind the eye with sparkling pomp and circumstance. No one wore clothes better than this king. Anne approached and curtseyed deeply, thinking that the sight of this still youthful sovereign sent every feminine heart racing with bedazzlement. Clothing made the man, and she wondered whether the instrument hiding within his codpiece was accordingly regal as well as his visual attributes. She had seen and spoken to him many times before king and cardinal had evicted her from court, but this encounter in 1526 seemed different, as if the sunlight had suddenly become more vivid and encompassing and was shining on a new day.

Henry spoke first, saying, 'Welcome back, Mistress Boleyn. You are needed to help the queen practice her French.'

'Oh God,' thought Anne, 'Not a word about the masque and dancing. All I am in his estimation is a French teacher to his dull wife; so much for lust and politics. I wonder if teaching French qualifies for politics? How boring.' Out loud she simply said: 'Whatever pleases you, Sire, is my command.'

'Well, in that case,' he countered, 'come to my chambers this evening so we may talk in private.'

Later that evening, Anne Boleyn was treading her way through the labyrinth of Greenwich Palace, headed for her first private meeting with the king. She viewed the building critically as she walked. It was almost twice as large as York Place and housed possibly a thousand people, who nobody bothered to count; all jammed together in chaotic but highly intimate manly living. She sensed that here was a home permeated with masculine boisterousness, athletic prowess, male truculence, and cut-throat competition. The females of the species were kept discreetly out of sight. It smelled of male semen and muscular sweat, horses and pack animals, over-cooked and rotting food, and an unpleasant mixture of perfume and sewage. A semblance of cleanliness was maintained around the king and his privy chambers where the dust was moved about regularly, the rushes on the floor replaced monthly and the laundry worked overtime. Elsewhere the tablecloths were black with grease, the drinking mugs unwashed, the meat lean, tough and old, and the cheese gnawed by rats and mice. Anne wondered why she was so anxious to give up Hever Castle for this codpiece-infested emporium.

Anne made her way through the great hall, up the central staircase, into the long gallery and a series of tandem antechambers before coming to the only closed and guarded door that opened into Henry VIII's private domain and his presence chamber. Here she acquired an escort. The rooms were smaller, the wood-panelled walls hung with rich tapestries depicting classical mythological scenes and the floors covered with those rarities, oriental carpets from Constantinople. Henry was sitting in an upholstered wooden armchair next to a refractory table laden with fruits and sweet-meats. He was listening to Giles Duwes, an accomplished lutenist who was just coming to the end of his performance. 'That was delightful,' the king praised his musician. 'Can you play a four-coursed instrument just as well as a three?' Before Duwes could answer, Anne stood at the open door, and Henry's interest in music vanished.

The king looked with unexpected delight at the young lady, framed by the ornate doorway as if she were about to step out of a picture. Her silken gown glimmered in the candlelight and her long, elegant neck displayed a face with luxuriant hair worn long, down below her bosom. He had never seen Anne without her hair coiffured tightly around her head and embellished by a wimple-like headdress, the height of fashion for the day. Her far less formal hairstyle both shocked and excited him and he immediately stepped forward and gave her a light kiss on the cheek, the traditional English signal for a warm welcome.

Henry could not explain the excitement he felt at viewing this dark beauty with rosebud lips and enticing eyes so beckoning; it wasn't as if Anne Boleyn was new to him. She had been at court as one of the queen's maids in waiting for at least five years and the king had heard her sing and had danced with her a multitude of times. So what was happening now? He marvelled whether it had anything to do with his having taken Mary Boleyn, now Mary Carey, as his mistress. Could his encounter with one sister have stimulated an interest in the other? Henry had a hard enough time maintaining a distinction between courtly and carnal love. The one led too easily into the other, and he found himself wanting to slay dragons and besiege castles to prove his courtly love for Anne but at the same time wondering whether she was the equal or better of her sister in naked bed. He suddenly felt that Anne might be something more than a potential bedmate; she might also be a future friend to whom he could lay bare his heart and talk about his marriage, his overly pious and dull wife, and his need for a male heir to keep his kingdom secure from civil war.

Anne was first to break what was fast becoming an awkward silence. 'Your Highness performed, as always, magnificently at the joust this afternoon, but why did you keep the visor of your helmet open? The Duke of Suffolk's spear missed your unprotected face by an inch. We all were aghast!'

'A stupid misadventure, and all my own fault. Forget it, and come and partake of the fruit and sweetmeats or order in anything you like better.'

At that moment the door opened and one of the king's ushers said, 'Your son, Henry Fitzroy, Duke of Richmond, has been struck down with a dangerously high fever, not the sweating sickness, thank God, and not contagious. He begs to speak with you.' The expression on the king's face was pure indecision; should he be a dutiful father or continue his dalliance with Mistress Boleyn? He chose the former, and turning to Anne said, 'I'm sorry but I must attend my son. We will meet again soon. I have much to talk about, and I am sure you will be a welcome listener.'

§

Anne and Henry were seated in a window alcove overlooking the southern lawn of Greenwich Palace; they were huddled over a chess table, scowling in concentration at an array of chessmen scattered over the board. Suddenly the king grunted, picked up his remaining bishop and moved it diagonally across the board, knocking Anne's knight off the table. 'There, that should block your advance for a while,' he said.

Anne answered nothing but a deep and wordless grin spread across her face. With a graceful movement of her arm she swept her queen across the board until it rested one square from Henry's king. 'Checkmate,' she murmured.

'Nonsense,' the king cried.

'You were greedy and fell into my trap,' she laughed.

Henry studied the board and finally said, 'Why can't I ever beat you? You cheat by distracting me with your delicate wrists, lovely fingers and succulent female presence. And what do you mean "I am greedy"? No one but you dares to call the king greedy.'

'Well if you hadn't been so anxious to destroy my knight you wouldn't have left your king unprotected. I call that being greedy.'

'I never have this trouble playing with the gentlemen of my privy chamber, and I regularly beat them.'

'Maybe they lose on purpose.'

'Yes, and it's very worrisome; they are nothing but sanctimonious flatterers. I sometimes allow them to win and they find it impossibly embarrassing.'

'Beating a king takes great courage and greater finesse.'

Henry ordered a round of ale, and as they waited he asked Anne whether she was aware that her father had petitioned him to save the life of a priest from Surrey who had been caught clipping gold coins. Anne begged ignorance, and the king explained the situation. 'It's an unusual case, probably more a matter of stupidity and naiveté than malice of forethought. The priest, whose name I cannot recall, owned an old angelot minted by Henry VI in Paris during the English occupation of the city in the Hundred Years' War. The coin had on one side the image of Saint Michael, which the priest wanted to turn into a religious medallion by filing off the outer rim of gold indicating that it was a coin of the realm. Then the silly man took the filed-off gold to a London goldsmith and tried to sell it. He was immediately arrested, and tried for having clipped and defaced royal currency. It happened so fast that nobody bothered to defrock him of his clerical status so technically he can still claim immunity from civil law through benefit of clergy. Had the angelot been coined at the royal mint in Winchester he would have been found not simply worthy of hanging but of a full traitor's execution, and if the judges had been my royal thirteenth-century ancestors he would have been flayed alive and his skin nailed to the doors of Westminster Abbey as a warning to the entire kingdom of the consequence of tampering with the coin of the realm. The fact that the angelot was minted in Paris raises the question whether it should be regarded as modern legal tender. What is your feminine take on the case? Should I pardon the idiot or not?'

Anne sipped her ale and answered, 'I think the issue of benefit of clergy is irrelevant. His actions clearly come under secular law. Moreover, I don't believe my father had any business concerning himself in what was none of his business, and as far as I am concerned you can hang the silly man; there are already far too many priests in the kingdom.'

Henry took a moment to digest this opinion, laughed and said: 'Some day someone is going to say that the female of the species is more ruthless than the male. I will do exactly as you advise.'

§

For all of 1526 Henry endured his growing infatuation more or less in secret. Anne was proving to be a most perceptive and understanding listener as he revealed his most privy thoughts. Katherine of Aragon, he admitted, was no longer a functioning wife, having long since ceased to menstruate. Instead she had grown cold and displeasing, shrinking into a closed shell of spiritual solitude. He had nothing left to say to her.

As he peered into the future he grew more and more alarmed at the thought of his maiden heir, the Princess Mary, being married off to an offspring of Charles, the Holy Roman Emperor, or François, the debauched King of France, and England reduced to a helpless Imperial or French province. The independent country of Brittany had already met such a fate, absorbed by France through marriage. Would his Plantagenet relatives, whom he reckoned by the dangerous dozen, or his illegitimate son Henry Fitzroy sit quietly and allow a foreign power to engross his kingdom, or would they individually or collectively try to seize the crown if only to prevent the land from becoming a foreign province?

Then there was the religious problem: how best to protect the country from the pernicious heresies spawned by Martin Luther. The king had already spoken his mind against the German pig in his bestselling *Assertio Septem Sacramentorum*, and now that Henry needed a separation from his elderly and unproductive wife, he expected an appreciative pope to be cooperative and understanding, and grant him an annulment without debate. There was much to talk about and Henry discovered that Anne had interesting and most unfeminine opinions on most of his problems. Her views on the Pope were far more critical than his own. In every way – in mind and body – he found Mistress Boleyn increasingly enthralling.

By the spring of 1527 Henry's quiet meetings with Anne had become common knowledge, and the queen had dismissed her as one of her maids of honour. This had made it difficult for Anne to remain at court and she was spending more and more time with her parents at Hever Castle. This in turn had forced Henry to do what he disliked most – write holograph letters in his own hand. Dictating love letters to a secretary seemed both inappropriate and intrusive. And so he sat at his desk staring at a sheet of blank paper, unable to phrase what his heart was demanding. Anne had been the perfect friend, demure and understanding, but what he desired was more, much more. He wanted her as his mistress. Friendship be damned! But how to express himself without risking feminine ire. He tested out a number of addresses: 'My sweetheart, my darling, my mistress, my beloved.' Not satisfied, he broke into poetry:

> Now unto my lady
> Promise to her I make,
> From all other only
> To her I me betake.

The words caught the spirit of his heart but were not the hot desires of a man grown young again.

He wrote in fluent French that was far better than his Spanish or Italian and the equal of his Latin. In fact the king was quite a linguist, complementing his musical talents. He read music at sight, composed it with grace and originality and loved nothing better than to accompany Anne in song or on the lute. He tried writing again; this time the words flowed with ardour: 'I and my heart commit ourselves into your hands, beseeching you to hold us recommended to your good favour, remembering that the longer the days are, the farther off is the sun, and yet, notwithstanding the hotter; so it is with our love, for we by absence are far sundered, yet it nevertheless keeps its fervency, at the least on my part, holding in hope the like on yours.' Such expressions of pain in her absence would do as a start, and he sent her his image in miniature set in the band of a golden bracelet, and ended the first of his seventeen letters to his dearly beloved with the closing expression: 'Your loyal and most ensured servant.' Then, thinking that these words did not transmit the heat of his sentiments, he added '*H autre AB ne cherche R*' [deciphered out of the French as Henry Rex seeks no other than Anne Boleyn. The sign of the heart surrounded the AB].

Henry's letter had not, of course, come to the real purpose of his literary efforts. Several more letters passed between them, and eventually he found the words to express his desires with brutal frankness. 'Debating with myself the contents of your letters, I have put myself in great distress, not knowing how to interpret them, whether to my advantage or disadvantage. I pray you with all my heart that you will expressly certify me of your whole mind concerning the love between us two. For of necessity I must ensure me of this answer, having been now above one whole year struck with the dart of love, not being assured either of failure or finding place in your heart. This truth has kept me from calling you my mistress, since if you love me in none other sort save that of common affection, the name of mistress, which denotes love of an exceptional kind, in no wise belongs to you. But if it shall please you to do me the office of a true, loyal mistress and friend, and give yourself up, body and soul, to me who will be and have been your very loyal servant, I promise you that not only shall the name be given you, but that I will take you for my mistress, rejecting from thought and affection all others save yourself, to serve you only.' Once started he could not stop, and he beseeched her to answer his 'rude letter' absolutely and in person, and not leave him in limbo. 'Written with the hand of that secretary who in heart, body and will is your loyal and most ensured servant.'

Anne feigned hard to get. She let him know that she was not pleased by his 'rude letter' with its *droit de seigneur* tone expecting Anne to rush into his bed at his command. The memory of her sister Mary's experiences with Henry Tudor still rankled. Was she now going to be the second Boleyn to be honoured beyond her wildest expectations and then quickly cast off? Moreover, she had come to know her king during those long evening conversations; she knew his foibles, his pride and his anger. Did she really want to regularise their relationship and grant him her body to do with what he chose? Her initial response was less than cordial. 'I think Your Majesty,' she wrote, 'speaketh these words in mirth to prove me, without intent of defiling your princely self. I have already given my maidenhead into my husband's hands.' The suggestion that she was saving herself and her chastity for some future husband was the sheerest fabrication. She had not forgotten the romps in the countryside with Henry Percy or the excitement in bed with Wyatt. It took Anne several months to make a decision but finally she found the promise of being permanent and sole mistress to the king too attractive to turn down. She sent him a gift, in French *une etrenne*, or New

Year's present, of a toy ship bearing a female passenger with a diamond about her neck. In the language of courtly love the meaning was manifestly clear: the boat symbolised the need to offer the lady eternal protection and the diamond spoke of the willingness of her heart. Henry was ecstatic; she would return to court his mistress for life.

§

Henry prided himself on having two bowling greens at his palace of Hampton Court: one on flat ground, the other on undulating and hilly land, but both beautifully manicured and evenly cut and usable during the early spring months. The hilly green was played with elliptical bowls with irregular sides to make them role in an arc and cling to the hillsides. Selecting the bowl with the proper bias was fifty per cent of the game. It made the sport doubly difficult. This morning only three men were playing on the level green: the king, Thomas Wyatt and Francis Weston. Henry bowled first, placing his ball within eight inches of the white marker ball; the closest bowl won. Wyatt was the second player and he equalled the king's shot, placing his bowl also eight inches from the marker. Their bowls were only inches apart and in front of the marker. This made for an almost impossible shot for Weston, who could not reach the marker without hitting one or the other of his opponent's bowls. Instead of conceding the game he went to where the elliptical bowls for a game on the hilly green were laid out, picked up a bowl and threw it at right angles to the level bowling green. He watched as the bowl circled and came to rest behind his opponents' two bowls, only inches from the white marker. It was a remarkable throw.

'Illegal,' cried Henry and Wyatt almost in unison. 'You can't mix bowls; they are separate games.'

'Not at all,' argued Weston. 'A bowling ball is a bowling ball.'

'Sorry,' announced the king, 'you are outvoted two to one. Come, Thomas. Let's go and measure our balls. I bet I am the closer.' They stood over their balls and Henry ostentatiously pointed at his ball with his little finger displaying a small love ring, the only digit small enough to carry the delicate ornament. Thomas immediately recognised it as belonging to Anne Boleyn. Every competitive instinct urged him to show the king that he possessed no monopoly over the lady. Was he a man or minion? At the same time every impulse warned him to be cautious; baiting a king was dangerous sport. Without hesitation Wyatt pulled out from his blouse the necklace he had purloined from Anne's neck months before. 'Here, let's measure with this.' He reached down and placed the chain between the marker and the king's bowl.

In his turn Henry recognised the trinket and drew the wrong conclusion; Anne had given the necklace to Wyatt as a love token. His complexion turned a brilliant red, and he swept up the ornamental chain in his huge hands and shouted, 'Where did you get this?'

Before Wyatt could answer he dropped the necklace and stalked off the bowling green. He had suddenly realised that if Thomas answered, he would have to admit to his serious interest in Anne, and he had promised the lady to keep his passions secret until she ordered otherwise. He would demand an explanation from his beloved. Why she insisted on keeping their mutual love a secret he did not understand; he was beginning to think that the light of his life was a control enthusiast. On his part, Wyatt realised he was in serious danger of getting in over his head. He quietly slipped away, thinking he might take a long vacation with Sir John Russell to Italy on diplomatic mission. The field was left to Henry Tudor; Anne belonged to him.

His Eminence, Cardinal Wolsey, sat at his desk with its top inlaid in mother-of-pearl and hinged to expose a storage space for unfinished letters and business papers. Here was the decision-making centre for both Church and State. The man who could humble and berate the most prestigious nobleman in the realm and force the Archbishop of Canterbury to do his bidding was seated, elbows on the tabletop, and his cupped hands supporting his chin. The effect was of an enormous crimson-gowned frog waiting for some unsuspecting fly to come into range of his tongue. In fact, the cardinal was not contemplating his next meal but meditating his future, which he found gloomy in the extreme. In the past, fortune's wheel had constantly turned in his favour, his life a constant success story; even his early disgraces and failures had concealed happy outcomes, as when he had been tutor and school teacher to the Marquis of Dorset's three sons, and Sir Amias Paulet, living nearby, had ordered him placed in the stocks because he found Wolsey to be pedantically arrogant and offensively intelligent. He had sat wrist and neck pinioned for a full day of uncomfortable mortification. Revenge had come in full measure when many years later as Lord Chancellor of England he had commanded Paulet to attend his council, delivered a lashing dressing-down, and ordered him on pain of forfeiture of all his property not to depart without licence, which was withheld for six years until the beleaguered man had purchased, rebuilt and turned over to the clerical Lord Chancellor a sumptuous house in London. Not a particularly Christian success story, but Wolsey was not a man who believed that forgiveness mixed well with success. From the moment he entered the service of the crown, fortune with her sugary smile had beamed upon him.

What disturbed him at the moment was a distinct feeling that fortune's wheel had ceased to revolve in his favour. Everything, even the most reasonable diplomatic decisions, seemed to be going wrong. He was not a happy man. He was contemplating not only the unexpected success of that 'midnight cow', as the cardinal always thought of Anne Boleyn, and her pernicious influence on the king but also the far greater disaster back in 1525 of the staggering French defeat at the Battle of Pavia and the subsequent sack of Rome by Imperial troops. Wolsey felt that he was indirectly responsible for both. War had broken out between François I of France and Charles V of the Hapsburg Empire largely because of the defection of Charles, Duke of Bourbon, the Constable of France and the country's greatest nobleman and therefore a potential threat to the King of France, who confiscated much of his property. Bourbon's answer was to join in military alliance with the Emperor Charles and make war on his king. This alliance was soon enlarged to include Henry VIII of England on the understanding that Henry would finance the duke and the emperor would supply the German troops, many of whom were Protestants.

The duke seized the Italian city of Pavia, but it soon became apparent that François was more than a match for his enemies. He surrounded Pavia with a far larger army and proposed to starve the duke into submission. As the siege progressed, Wolsey and his king decided that Bourbon would eventually be defeated and cut off the supply of money to pay his army. This led Bourbon to an act of desperation: he planned and executed a night frontal attack with a small, handpicked cadre of men against the French artillery besieging the city's main gate. Their attack was furious and effective, and they captured the French cannon, which they promptly turned around and pointed at the French army. Then Bourbon's main force of some 16,000 men exited the city by its side gates and attacked the French camp where the bulk of the French army was still soundly asleep.

The result was cataclysmic. François and most of the French military leaders were caught and captured in their sleeping gowns, and the army thrown into leaderless confusion. The camp tents and all the cannon were seized, and Bourbon decided to move his triumphant army on to Rome, offering his unpaid and hungry troops the loot of the city as recompense. Not since the days of Nero playing music while his city burned had Rome endured such a nightmare. Imperial soldiers ransomed, slaughtered, and tortured civilians at will; the populace rose up against the wealthy, plundering their riches and priceless possessions; stories were reported of ghastly scenes of babies being skewered on stakes and barbequed to death; and the Pope took refuge in Castel Sant'Angelo, the only defensible building in the city. Had Wolsey not cut off funding for the Duke of Bourbon, the Battle of Pavia would never have been fought, Rome not plundered and ravished, the Pope not made absolutely dependent for the protection of his papal states on the emperor, and Charles V not made quite by accident the Leviathan of Europe. No loss of a horseshoe could match Wolsey's miscalculations in terms of consequences, and all to save the English exchequer a few thousand pounds sterling. All this just at the moment that Anne Boleyn was entrancing Henry VIII with her wit and sex appeal.

The full consequences of Pavia took a while for the king and cardinal to realise. At first it seemed to be a miraculous victory, leaving that despicable roué François a miserable captive and the English friend and ally the Emperor Charles the champion of Europe. The fact that he was also Katherine of Aragon's nephew and had a highly developed sense of family solidarity and honour soon became dreadfully apparent. Worse, he commanded all of Italy and the Pope had suddenly become an Imperial chaplain ready and willing to do the emperor's bidding.

Wolsey sensed that the situation was even worse than most people imagined; fortune's wheel was frowning and everything that could go wrong was going from bad to worse because his king was showing three dangerous signs of independent thinking that the cardinal had no way of controlling. Henry's conscience had suddenly been inflamed by words in the book of Leviticus that his seventeen-year marriage to his wife Katherine was illegal in the minds of both God and man, he was in the throes of falling in love with a commoner who bore the cardinal great ill-will but who had no idea how to behave or think like a queen, and the king had now reached the age of discretion and was accepting the gruelling work of kingship. He was thirty-six and ready to be a working monarch without benefit of his cardinal legate.

Wolsey knew all about Henry's conscience; in fact he may have accidently stirred up the monster by suggesting he read Leviticus when he started to complain that his wife had failed in her duty as a queen to produce a male heir to the throne, had given him nothing but stillbirths and frail infants who died within the month, and was now beyond the conceiving age. She was forty-one, five years Henry's senior, and although he was fond of Katherine, his marriage was nonetheless one of convenience not love. He might also add that she was totally absorbed in prayer and spiritual meditation. They no longer had anything in common except their daughter Mary, who might very well lead the kingdom into civil war once Henry was in his grave, for Henry had an illegitimate son, Henry Fitzroy, who as the only male Tudor might make a bid for the throne.

His Eminence rose slowly to his feet, each pound of his massive body a challenge to his aging command. His mental homily had been lengthy to the point of tedium. He needed human contact and response to conjure up and control the future. He went to the door of his chambers, opened it and shouted, 'Get Thomas Cromwell here at once.' As soon as Cromwell appeared he was confronted with a question: 'Will the Pope grant me an annulment of this marriage on the basis of Leviticus 20:21?' The cardinal knew that Thomas could recite the Bible from memory.

Cromwell took a moment to answer, then said, 'Your Grace knows canon law far better than I.'

Wolsey brushed the answer aside with a wave of his hand and said, 'True, but I need the opinion of a well-educated layman.'

'Then my answer must be no, he would not grant such an annulment. I don't blame the king for thinking that Leviticus speaks to his problem: it says "If a man shall take his brother's wife it is an unclean thing … he shall be without children," which appears to fit the royal situation perfectly. The trouble is that the Bible is not consistent: Deuteronomy decrees the opposite – "When brothers dwell together, and one of them dieth without children, the wife of the deceased shall not marry to another; but his brother shall take her, and raise up seed for his brother." The two statements are in open conflict. For the king's argument to succeed Deuteronomy must be explained away, and that would entail a bitter exegetic war between clerical scholars who will find not according to the truth but for whoever holds the purse strings or yields the sharpest sword.'

'Alas, I agree. So what is to be done?'

'Since the king's marriage to his deceased brother's wife required a papal dispensation in the first place, only the Pope can grant a nullification by eating previous papal words and admitting his predecessor had been wrong in having granted a dispensation to revoke Leviticus and permit the marriage. This he does not want to do for fear of antagonising the Emperor Charles. Worse, as a de Medici he is feeling particularly insecure because the city of Florence has recently rebelled against his family and thrown the de Medici out of power. Only force will prevail. We must beg and threaten at the same time. I would send him a grand petition signed by every ranking clergyman and nobleman begging him to grant the annulment to warn him that every important person in the kingdom favours an annulment. Imbedded in the petition should be wording suggesting that if our pleas fails there are other and more violent options available to England. The Church can be torn asunder by the King's Great Matter.'

'A long speech, Cromwell, but pregnant; let's try your suggestion. If it doesn't work, which I don't think it will, we will tighten the screws and cut off the money supply to the Vatican. A de Medici pope is always in need of cash. This is where your membership in Parliament will be indispensable.'

§

The winter of 1527–28 ebbed and swirled at its usual erratic pace, one day chaotic with excitement, the next as dull as hunting rabbits, but throughout the seasons Cupid's arrows were pricking ever deeper into the king's consciousness drugging him with love's passions. Wolsey spent most of the summer on a grand but futile tour of French hospitality trying to undo the calamity of the French defeat at Pavia and visiting a Pope in self-imposed captivity in Castel Sant'Angelo, proclaiming that he would live and die an imperialist doing the emperor's bidding. The cardinal wanted French assistance in organising a Church council favourable to Henry's marital needs to coerce the Pope into a more favourable stance on the King's Great

Matter. In this he failed and discovered that his king was negotiating directly with Pope Clement without telling him. The only thing left for Wolsey to do was to spend his time wining and dining with the French king and complaining that although the French monarch and aristocracy were pleasant enough, the French populace still remembered and hated the English for their horrific behaviour burning, raping, and stringing up French priests by the neck for the pleasure of seeing them dangle and struggle for breath during the last years of the Hundred Years' War. The French expressed their ire by stealing all of the cardinal's possessions, which were not locked away or guarded by armed soldiers.

The only Englishmen to really enjoy the French gambol were Mark Smeaton and George Cavendish. The former experienced French cordiality when Wolsey's travelling choir of songsters so impressed the French king that he begged the cardinal to lend them to him for a few days' exhibition. As a result Mark was treated and dined as if he were a duke and French damsels were happy to open wide their skirts to his lustful advances.

Cavendish fell into a different kind of love. He was scouting the town of Compiègne for places for his cardinal to sleep the following day. His horse cast its shoe and in the process of finding a blacksmith he met the servants of the Count de Cerci who resided in a nearby fairytale castle. The count was of royal blood and lavish hospitality, and was anxious to meet, dine and house for the night this servant of the English cardinal. Cavendish was met by the count's family and household servants all dressed in black coats and gowns, standing in regimental order. He was led first into the great hall, its wall festooned with hand guns, then into the parlour hung with fine tapestries, the count boasting of the defensive strength of his castle and taking him on a tour of his castle with its fifteen-foot-thick walls and cannon already charged with shot should the French king and English cardinal condescend to stop next day at his residence. Cavendish was profoundly impressed by the wealth and luxury on display, especially the magnificent Spanish chargers or jennets ridden by twelve of the count's pages of honour, all clothed in coats of gold and black velvet, boots of red Spanish leather and gilded spurs. No English nobleman could match such opulence.

While the cardinal was prancing about France in a grandiose but fruitless style, King Henry had been in contact with Pope Clement and had arranged that the Pope should send Cardinal Lorenzo Campeggio to England to establish a marital court with Cardinal Wolsey to adjudicate and annul the king's marriage. What the English negotiators had failed to achieve was a commission from His Holiness accepting any decision by the court as final. Unmentioned was the possibility of an appeal back to Rome as the highest court in Christendom.

The arrival of Campeggio in London in October changed both the tempo and substance of the King's

Great Matter. Henry determined that Anne was no longer simply his mistress but now that an annulment of his first marriage was imminent, he began to think about her as a future wife, and this caused a problem for both of them that had to be resolved. The existence of carnal love placed in jeopardy any decision of the court to grant him an annulment on the basis of conscience. The opposition could argue that the king's conscientious conviction that his marriage to Katherine was illegal and displeasing to God must be dismissed as mere cover-up for lust for another woman. Henry knew that the legal annulment of his marriage had to precede any official engagement to Anne, and therefore they had to stop all fornication between them. This, he realised, had to be the price paid for remarriage and a new queen. The great question remained, what did Anne want? Mistress or queen? Henry could not imagine that Anne would refuse marriage and queenship, but did they both have sufficient self-restraint to live in close proximity without the pleasures of copulation?

They met in the king's closet to discuss the future of their love and all its political and dynastic implications. Two naked bodies in a mammoth bed, even Henry's massive body seemed overwhelmed by the royal couch as wide as it was long and supporting a canopy displaying the king's coat of arms. Henry was on his elbows looking down at Anne's welcoming and expectant lips. 'Anne,' he murmured, 'you are the most ravishing creature ever to adorn my bed, a veritable

Helen of Troy whose magic is beyond that of all the Medes and Persians combined. You entrance, thrill, and confound me by your every glance. I am melted wax in your hands. Sweet Anne, your lips suck forth my soul and leave me helpless in the heaven of your love. You are chained to me forever as my precious paramour.'

Anne pushed Henry's monumental frame off her chest and ordered him to cease his lovesick babbling. 'We must stop these pleasant but fruitless words and plan ahead. What you want is another night of fornication; what we need is a decision on whether I should continue to be your mistress, or am I to be your bride?'

'Eventually I profoundly hope so; nothing would make me happier than to lead you down the aisle of Westminster Abbey, but for the moment your name must be removed from the marital court's mind. Nothing must interfere with a favourable decision of my annulment. The annulment has nothing to do with my love for you. Remarriage is less important to me than the legitimacy of my future children. I might very well defy His Holiness, go it alone and marry whom I please but nothing but a papal annulment of my mis-marriage to Katherine can make any future children we might have legitimate. I already have two illegitimate offspring, the Princess Mary and the Duke of Richmond, a third would be intolerable. That is why I cling to the Pope. It has nothing to do with religion or faith or being an obedient son of the

Church. As Sir Thomas More once warned me, the Pope is only a man, not a deity. The trouble is that the future existence of my dynasty lies in his hands. He alone controls the fate of my kingdom, and I have every reason to expect a favourable decision by the court. He owes me.'

'Are kings of England now inferior to the Pope?' asked Anne. 'Do they have superior power to the divine and historic majesty of English monarchs to do as they please in a London court of law? And aren't you being overly optimistic about the Pope's actions? Ever since the Battle of Pavia and the sack of Rome he has been the captive of the emperor, who has made it perfectly clear that he will never allow a legal replacement of his aunt, that tub of Spanish pride, your wife. Wolsey and Campeggio are about to go through a display of papal and legal contortionism that will only further obscure the issue of your marriage, not resolve it. It is silly to worry about the legitimacy of any children until you have a legal wife.'

'Either way, my sweet, legal children or legal wife, we must cease being copesmates in naked bed and return to the ancient ceremonies of courtly love.'

'And what if Campeggio has secret orders from Rome to postpone any decision and hang the court?'

'Then we apply greater pressure,' replied the king. 'We ally with France and cast Charles out of Italy by force of arms and return the Pope to a free agent, or we threaten to cut all financial ties between England and Rome and drive His Holiness into bankruptcy, which he can ill afford, especially now that the de Medici family has been expelled from Florence. Let us wait and see what Wolsey and Campeggio can achieve and then settle on whether I am a mistressless lover nurturing a future bride or a satisfied paramour with every intent to keep his mistress satisfied in body and soul.'

Anne was less than happy with such a formulation of choices, but she had set her heart and career on becoming queen, and physical desire, no matter how urgent, was not going to interfere with her long-term plans; sex had always been a tool, never an end in itself. She even considered speaking to her sister-in-law about a few words with the devil to influence the papal proceedings. So given these choices, she also elected abstinence. Henry's mind was obviously still on foining, either delayed for the sake of future legitimacy or preferably that very moment to consummate present desires, and he suggested that 'since we are to cease copulation, and "the standing prick has no conscience," we should indulge ourselves in a final orgasm of sexual pleasure'. Celibacy was always more tolerable when postponed a few minutes.

Wolsey rose early that morning to arrange for the king's marital trial the next day at Blackfriars. It was like organising his own execution, he thought; not for a moment did he believe that the Pope had granted him or

Campeggio full powers to try the case without appeal to Rome, and he suspected that the Italian cardinal had secret orders from the pontiff to derail the case. He also surmised it was dangerous to underestimate Katherine; she might look like a fat frumpish washerwoman but the cardinal well knew she concealed the pride of a dozen Spaniards from Aragon and had a built-in sense of the dramatic. Despite the king's optimism about the outcome of the trial, Wolsey expected the worst, and shuddered to think of a hung or negative decision. His credibility with the king would be shattered and the jackals and wolves that had resented his leadership for the past eighteen years would soon be gathering.

The great hall at Blackfriars had to be transformed into a courtroom with a raised dais for the two cardinals, a throne chair replete with cloth of estate for Henry, a lesser chair nearby for the queen, seats in front of Wolsey and Campeggio for the lesser judicial officers, seating for bishops Sampson and Fisher, respectively the king's and queen's counsels at opposite ends of the hall, and more benches reserved for the English episcopate of bishops and abbots headed by the Archbishop of Canterbury. Anne, along with the dukes of Norfolk and Suffolk, were placed in the minstrel gallery at the end of the hall; the trial was a Church affair and it was best to keep the temporal authority out of sight.

The court opened proceeding on the eighteenth of June 1529 by reading the Pope's commission to the judges and demanding the presence of King Henry of

England. As the king seated himself, the queen was called. Instead of taking the chair assigned her she marched over to her husband, knelt before him and spoke words for the entire company to hear:

'Sir, I beseech you for all the loves that hath been between us and the love of God, let me have justice and right; take of me some pity and compassion, for I am a poor woman and a stranger, born out of your dominion. I have here no assured friends and much less impartial counsel. I take God and all the world to witness that I have been to you a true, humble, and obedient wife being always well pleased and contented with all things wherein ye have any delight or dalliance; I never grudged in word or countenance or showed a visage or spark of discontentment. I loved all those whom ye loved only for your sake whether they were my friends or enemies.

'And when ye had me at the first (I take God to be my judge) I was a true maid without touch of man. The king your father and my father Ferdinand, King of Spain, were both wise and excellent kings in wisdom and princely behaviour. Is it not therefore to be doubted but that they elected and gathered as wise counsellors about them as their high discretions thought meet, all of whom viewed the marriage between you and me to be good and lawful. Therefore it is a wonder to me what new inventions are now directed against me who never intended anything except honesty, and caused me to stand before this court where it is impossible for me to receive a fair hearing. You must realise that my counsel are your subjects and dare not for your displeasure disobey your will and intent. I beg of you, before this court gives a decision, to allow me enough time to ask my friends in Spain for impartial advice as to what kind of defence to make. If out of cruelty you do not see fit to do so, I then to God commit my case.'

With this final threat she rose, curtsied as deeply as her stout body would allow, and stalked out of the hall and building, ignoring all orders for her to return and take her seat. The queen's words and actions had been well rehearsed, and it was clear to all that she was reciting ideas coined by her chief counsellor, John Fisher, the aged but ferocious Bishop of Rochester and Katherine's most passionate champion. Only Henry had the nerve to speak to the prolonged silence that followed the queen's departure. He sought, by praising Katherine and their marriage, to undo some of the harm the queen had achieved to his chances of winning an annulment. 'For as much as the queen has gone,' he announced, 'I will declare unto all my lords here presently assembled that she has been to me as true, obedient, and comfortable a wife as I could in my fondest fancy wish or desire. She is a noble woman born as her manner and bearing this day clearly confirms.'

Wolsey finally found his tongue, anxious to take advantage of the king's unexpectedly gracious mood. 'Your Grace, I most humbly beseech you to declare to this audience whether I was the chief inventor or first mover for questioning the legality of your marriage to the queen.'

'My lord cardinal,' spoke the king, 'I can well excuse you herein. Marry indeed; ye have been rather against me in attempting or setting forth thereof. To put you all out of doubt I shall reveal the first cause of my prick of conscience and first questioning the validity of my marriage. It was the French ambassador negotiating a possible marriage between the Duke of Orleans, the king's son, and my daughter, the Princess Mary, who questioned the princess's legitimacy because of the queen's previous marriage to my brother Prince Arthur. He thought possibly that Mary was illegitimate. These words pricked my conscience and so disquieted my mind that I was in great doubt of God's indignation. Divine punishment was clear: all male issue died at birth or soon after. Troubled by waves of scrupulous conscience and despair over lack of a son to inherit the imperial dignity, I thought it best for my kingdom to test the legality of my marriage and discover whether my copulation with Katherine had been unlawful these past twenty years. My purpose had nothing to do with any carnal concupiscence or displeasure with my queen or her age but only with a quest for truth and relief of a troubled mind.'

When Henry had finished his soliloquy, William Warham, Archbishop of Canterbury, made the mistake of rising and saying that the entire episcopal bench agreed with the king's interpretation of God's law and his right to dissolve his marriage. 'I doubt not that but all my brethren here present will affirm the same.' At which point John Fisher shouted, 'No, sir, not I, ye have not my consent thereto.' This produced a long and embarrassing squabble between bishop and archbishop until the king intervened. 'Well, well, it shall make no matter. We will not waste time in argument for the bishop is but one man, standing alone in opposition.' At this point the court, its agenda and credibility already badly scarred, adjourned for the day.

After another session of footless argument, Wolsey retired to York Place exhausted and went to bed. Two hours later he was abruptly awakened by the newly ennobled Baron Rochford, Anne's father, Thomas Boleyn, who had been sent by the king with orders that Wolsey and Campeggio must go immediately to the queen and persuade her to withdraw from the trial and leave the entire matter in the king's hands, which would be much better for her than continuing to debate Church law and running the risk of being condemned. Wolsey ordered up his barge and picked up Campeggio, both men arriving in the evening to find the queen with a skein of white thread about her neck busily sewing with her ladies in waiting. The cardinals asked for a private interview and Katherine countered, 'My lords if ye have anything to say, speak it openly before all these folk, for I fear nothing that ye can say or allege against me, but that I would all the world should both hear and see it.' Wolsey then broke into Latin but the queen insisted on English, which she spoke badly but understood perfectly. Wolsey was insistent on keeping their interview private and said that if the queen wanted to hear their secret opinions on her marriage it would have to be done in her private chambers.

Their conversation was prolonged and intense but no one in the adjacent rooms could hear what was being said although the queen spoke as loudly as she could. Even after twenty years of adaptation, Katherine was unable to get her tongue to come forth with understandable English; she spoke with a heavy Spanish accent. 'I am going to surprise you. I have,' she said, 'a bargain to make with Henry. I will relinquish my crown, and retire into a nunnery. Life in a house of God cannot be very different from my present existence surrounded by my ladies in waiting but in effect I am isolated from the outside world.' Both cardinals heartily agreed.

'BUT,' she continued, emphasising the word, 'there is one absolute and non-negotiable condition: my daughter, the Princess Mary, would have to be acknowledged both by Act of Parliament and by royal proclamation to be the king's legal heir to the throne, taking precedent over all future children.' She smiled sweetly as she spoke.

The proposal left both cardinals speechless. Wolsey found his voice first: 'Madame, you cannot expect us to take such a message to the king. He will reject the idea out of hand and I shudder to think what Mistress Boleyn will say; her language is even richer than the king's.'

'We fear for our lives,' added Campeggio.

Amused by their reactions, Katherine patiently explained to the prelates: 'My bargain is easy to achieve and not particularly unusual. There is no need to worry about your lives. My husband can be very sensible if he sets his mind to it. Canon law requires that any infant born to a marriage, thought by the parents to be legal, remains legitimate even when the union has later been found to be invalid. Anyone conceived in good faith, as Mary surely was, can rightfully claim legitimacy.'

Both cardinals acknowledged the queen's argument but Wolsey went on to point out that 'English common law does not recognise canon law.'

'Simple,' Katherine countered, 'then have Parliament change the law. Not in the least difficult for a divinely inspired monarch to do.'

Wolsey and Campeggio left the queen's chambers arguing which one would bear the queen's prickly proposal to Henry. Campeggio argued that since Wolsey was the senior cardinal it was his duty; Wolsey rebutted that Campeggio as a young man had been married and was better equipped to handle a marital dispute. In the end both bearded the dangerous lion in his den at Greenwich Palace with predictable result. Henry refused the queen's terms with a string of oaths that Wolsey had never heard the king use before; he adamantly declined to even mention the subject to Anne, and announced that no court or pope could ever force him to live with his troubled conscience unrelieved.

At the final session of the court the king sat in the minstrel's gallery and ordered his council to call for final judgment. Campeggio rose and pronounced: 'I will give no judgment herein until I have made relation unto the Pope of all our proceedings, whose counsel and commandment in this high case I will observe. The case is too high, and too well known throughout the world, for us to give any hasty judgment, considering the highness of the persons and doubtfulness of the allegations involved. Wherefore I will adjourn this court according to the Roman calendar that calls for a recess until next Bartholomew-tide, the twenty-fourth of August.'

The wolves and jackals scarcely waited, as Wolsey had predicted, for Campeggio to finish adjourning the court before they appeared on the scene. Charles Brandon, the Duke of Suffolk and the king's brother-in-law, had been standing next to the king. He stepped forward, and in a loud and caustic voice and even more arrogant countenance bellowed, 'It was never merry in England whilst we had cardinals among us.' The words were typical of the duke, who possessed a choleric temperament, never giving thought to the consequences of his words or actions. In the silence that ensued Wolsey felt obliged to speak up. 'My lord, hold your peace, and pacify yourself, and frame your tongue like a man of honour and wisdom, and not to speak so quickly or so reproachfully of your friends.' The cardinal's words silenced the duke but not the displeasure of the king, who continued to blame his cardinal for the Blackfriar fiasco.

What followed was natural to royal government, where all success and failure depended on access to the king's ear. The cardinal was detested by the two most ranking noblemen of the realm – the dukes of Norfolk and Suffolk – who coveted for themselves all influence over the king, despised the cardinal's humble birth, and regarded him an arrogant upstart. The animosity of Anne Boleyn and her father, shortly to become the Earl of Wiltshire, for Cardinal Wolsey was equally well known, and they were just as anxious as the two dukes to isolate Wolsey from his royal master. Anne was in the most favoured position as she dined regularly with Henry and could excite his passion for the hunt and keep him from meeting up with his most experienced and intelligent servant.

The result was soon manifest; Norfolk and Suffolk took a barge to York Place with written instructions from the king to dismiss the cardinal from his office of Lord Chancellor, return the Great Seal to the king, and commandeer York Place and Hampton Court as now belonging to the monarch and being far too magnificent for a man only a cardinal in name and only Archbishop of York in fact. Wolsey's enemies all agreed that he belonged nowhere near his sovereign but in his archiepiscopal headquarters in Yorkshire, as far from London and the centre of politics as he could reasonably be sent.

George Cavendish, Mark Smeaton and Thomas Cromwell were all seated in the main dining hall of Esher House, a miniscule residence compared to York Place but the only property the cardinal possessed close to London and the royal court. It belonged to the diocese of Winchester, but since Wolsey among his many ecclesiastical titles was Bishop of Winchester, none of his many enemies at court could legitimately protest that the detested cardinal was dangerously close to London and to Hampton Court, which Henry was beginning to use more and more frequently. A skeleton of servants was all that was left of the multitude that had served him at York Place, and to make Esher serviceable the cardinal had had to borrow bedding, cutlery and dishes from the neighbouring and accommodating Sir Thomas Arundel.

The three friends were discussing their master's disgrace and catastrophic fall from power and their own dubious future. Who or what was responsible? Cavendish belaboured Anne Boleyn, maintaining that the lady was vengeful and vindictive, was in league with Satan, and had never forgiven or forgotten the cardinal's ruination of her marriage to the future Earl of Northampton. 'She spends her days pouring poison into the king's ear and inflaming her father's, and the dukes of Norfolk and Suffolk dislike of the parvenu cleric.' Mark tended to agree but surmised that fate in the form of fortune's wheel was to blame. Cromwell was more prosaic but more reflective, suggesting that neither God nor woman were answerable; their master's fall was the king's decision. The king had lost confidence in his cardinal, was suspicious of his motives, which he felt were anti-Boleyn in general and anti-Anne in particular, and he no longer needed an alter rex to relieve him of the drudgery of kingship.

'Our analyses are all very well,' interrupted Smeaton, 'but what are we going to do about it? For whom will I sing for my supper in the future? Thomas, you have spent your time looking after His Eminence's parliamentary and real-estate affairs, dissolving twenty-nine small but wealthy monasteries in order to generate money to support Wolsey's precious colleges at Oxford and Ipswich. Can your private business and financial dealings survive without the cardinal's support? I am not at all sure. And you George, you worship the great man. Have you a future life?'

A long and uncomfortable silence ensued as the friends meditated what fate might have in store for them. Cromwell finally turned to Mark and said, 'You have an angelic voice and can get a position anywhere. I wager the King of France, having already heard you sing, is as of this moment making enquiries about your availability. And don't forget all those adoring French damsels. As for you, George, you are the luckiest of us all; you have wife, children and estates to return to. You can forsake the political life and become a quiet country gentleman. You will be happy in the countryside.'

'It sounds pleasant but deadly dull,' countered Cavendish.

'True,' acknowledged Thomas, 'but without the cruelty, bickering and desperate rivalry of court and city life. I am a widower and far too old to start afresh. I can only dream of the quiet and secure country life, but I am not a gentleman. Worse, I am a man hated throughout the kingdom. Many of the tasks assigned me by the cardinal demanded actions that were not exactly legal, and the country is swarming with people waiting for His Eminence to fall so they can stretch my neck. I am the least enviable of us all. I have made my life the cardinal's success story and now my prop and stay is a sick old man ready to die. My only hope is to make myself as indispensable to the king as I have been to the cardinal. I plan to leave for London to talk to my merchant friends, warn my household that I may soon be poverty stricken, and marshal my allies at court. Possibly even speak to the king. "Make or break" will be my motto.'

Cavendish rose from the table to attend to his master and said goodbye. Smeaton and Cromwell sat in communal silence until Smeaton said, 'Thomas, explain to me the Act of Praemunire and the cardinal's entanglement with it.'

'Not an easy request,' sighed Cromwell. 'It all goes back to the fourteenth century, when Parliament passed legislation preventing a foreign power, meaning the papacy, from doing two things: one, appointing anyone it chose, foreigner or native, to Church offices without regard to the right of free elections possessed by the English Church; and two, prohibiting the operation of all papal fiscal and legal jurisdiction in England without royal consent. As the centuries passed these sanctions were largely forgotten, and our master, the cardinal, had no trouble in accepting the papal decree of legatine authority that was technically a violation of English law. Moreover, he received the king's licence in his own hand and under the royal seal to exercise the legatine power throughout the kingdom. He has those documents hidden away somewhere. So you see when Parliament tried to pass a Bill of Attainder against the cardinal and his legatine powers, the king felt obliged to squelch the effort and kill the impeachment.'

'What would happen if these documents you speak about fell into the king's hands and he concealed them?' Mark asked.

'Our master would be hopelessly vulnerable, for then his excuse would only be a matter of hearsay; his word against the king's. And who would believe a disgraced royal servant?'

'Had he been attainted by Parliament what would his punishment have been? Death?'

'No, not capital punishment, but loss of all civil rights, forfeiture of all lands, goods and chattels, and imprisonment at the royal pleasure.'

'Very interesting, and it is just possible, Thomas, that I can help you, for I think I know where the cardinal keeps his most valuable papers.'

'Indeed, and where might that be?'

'You know of Wolsey's insistence that whenever he travels overnight he always takes his four-poster bed and his mother-of-pearl topped desk with the legs as heavy as a charwoman?'

'Vividly.'

'Well, the right front leg is hollow and conceals his most precious papers. I know this from long ago. As a child in the children's choir I was playing hide-and-go-seek and I hid in the cardinal's study. While I was hiding, the cardinal entered, sat at his desk and opened up the right-hand front leg. I saw and remembered exactly how he did it, and I still remember.'

'What's your price, Mark?'

'To what use will you put the documents?'

'That I cannot say for sure. Possibly I will give them to the Duke of Norfolk who now heads the king's council and detests the cardinal. If I can get an audience with the king I will turn them over to him. They rightfully belong to him.'

'You realise that what is being suggested is outright theft.'

'I've done worse. Again, Mark, your price?'

'Find me a secure place among the king's singers and musicians, and after you have won His Majesty's confidence and high office, I would gladly accept an annual New Year's gift. My singing wages will be insufficient to maintain myself as a gentleman.'

'It's a bargain; give me your hand to shake on it, and we will meet this night in his study after His Eminence is asleep, and I will head next day on horseback for London, armed with the keys to a new career for both of us.'

'And what about His Eminence?'

'He is a cagy article and will find a way out of his difficulties. I may betray him but I will not forsake him. I owe him too much.'

Mark listened to Thomas's words, and quietly wondered whether his friend liked to play semantic games with himself. How much difference was there between forsaking and betraying?

Cromwell returned next day from London with an eager spring in his gait. 'The king,' he told Smeaton, 'called me a knave but a useful scoundrel. His Majesty had been worried about the existence of these documents and wanted to get hold of them. He will get in touch with me in a few days. What happened here today?'

'As you might expect, the cardinal went to his desk, checked his precious papers and had a fit. He turned a pasty white, went to his private closet and I think wrote the king a letter. We will soon find out what it said because George was with him.'

Later that day Cavendish reported what the cardinal had penned. It was total surrender, confessing that he deserved the punishment reserved for those attainted for violating the Statute of Praemunire even though all legal action against him had been dropped. He turned over all his goods, property and chattel to his sovereign to do with as he pleased, and threw himself upon the mercy of the king, saying that he would rather do this than ever suggest that his only sin had been his eagerness to do his monarch's bidding in exercising his legatine powers. Henry was delighted, for he got York Place without the fight he had half expected, since the property belonged to the archdiocese of York, not to the cardinal as a private individual. The only reprimand his aging servitor dared deliver was to remind Henry that 'both heaven and hell' had to be reckoned with. The cardinal would, he wrote, since it was the king's pleasure, leave immediately for York and attend to his duties as archbishop. It would be the first time since his elevation to the office sixteen years before that he had ever set foot in his archdiocese. This time he did not take either his bed or desk on his travels, and both Mark Smeaton and Thomas Cromwell stayed behind. The faithful Cavendish accompanied his master into exile.

Wolsey and Cavendish travelled north as far as Cawood Castle, only seven miles south of York. Here he began preparation for his much-delayed enthronement as archbishop in York cathedral. However, all planning came to an abrupt and unexpected end when Henry Percy, now Sixth Earl of Northumberland, arrived just at the dinner hour on the fourth of November with a warrant for Wolsey's arrest for high treason. The meeting of cardinal and earl after six years was unimaginably awkward; Wolsey babbled feigned welcome and Northumberland was tongue-tied, unable to state his real reason for being there. With trembling legs he finally managed to whisper, 'My lord, I arrest you of high treason.' Wolsey was 'marvellously astonished,' and both men stood silently looking at one another. The cardinal composed himself first and asked, 'By whose authority?'

'I have a commission to warrant my doings' was Percy's inadequate reply.

'Let me see it.'

'Nay, sir that I may not.'

'Well then,' was His Eminence's quiet rejoinder, 'I will not obey your arrest unless you show me your written orders.' Northumberland remained silent, not knowing what to do. At this juncture Sir Walter Walsh, who had arrived in Northumberland's company, appeared before Wolsey on bended knee. Again the cardinal's outraged voice exclaimed that young Percy had come to arrest him but refused to display a commission. 'If you be privy to this idiocy and be joined with him in authority, kindly show me your papers.'

'It is true he has written orders but I beseech Your Grace to hold us excused; there is annexed unto our commission a schedule of instructions that you may in no wise be allowed to see.'

Since Wolsey recognised Walsh as a member of the king's privy chamber, he decided to accede to Walsh's refusal, and said, 'I am content to yield unto you but not to my Lord of Northumberland unless I see his commission. Your position in the king's privy chamber in itself even without a commission gives you the authority to arrest me, for the lowest person in the realm may arrest the greatest peer if the king so commands.'

George Cavendish had been singled out at the king's order to act as the cardinal's chief aide in arranging for His Eminence's armed escort to accompany him on the long trek back to London and imprisonment in the Tower. Cavendish's devotion and loyalty to his master was well known and admired at court, and he made the harrowing journey on the part of a sick and dying old man as comfortable as possible. The charges against Wolsey were mostly based on hearsay and surmise on the part of his political enemies who claimed that he had secretly conspired with the Pope and emperor to regain his lost authority in England. This, they argued, was tantamount to treason. Fortunately for his opponents the truth of these allegations was never tested, for His Eminence died, possibly of cancer, at Leicester Abbey at eight in the morning on November the twenty-ninth, 1530. He had come to the abbey, he said in a voice so weak few could hear him, 'to leave his bones amongst its monks.' His final words were an indictment of both his life and his king: 'Had I served God as diligently as I have done the king, He would not have given me over in my grey hairs.'

CHAPTER III

Sex and Revolution

It was the first of January 1531, one of those unexpectedly mild and sunny days in the dead of winter with the tantalising hint of spring whispering in the air. A lone peacock butterfly, flapping its gorgeous red wings with four dark blue round eyes embedded in the four corners, fluttered by, fooled by the warm weather. Cromwell and Smeaton were strolling in the king's privy garden at Hampton Court Palace while the king played tennis with Francis Weston. The two men had not met since they parted after the cardinal's death. Smeaton viewed the butterfly with compassion. The helpless creature was alone and vulnerable in a predatory world, rather like himself. They both needed protectors and both favoured gaudy clothing by way of defiance. Smeaton was bedecked in velvet indigo tights and maroon jacket with interchangeable sleeves; today one was greenish, the other light blue. He looked at Cromwell in his drab cloak and colourless clothing with a sense of deep affection and protection.

Thomas liked his young friend, whose mind was as sharp as his voice and his musical talents abounded. Cromwell had been to court on a daily basis ever since his initial meeting with the king. Henry had found him to be a charming and highly articulate scoundrel well versed in most of the more nefarious branches of sixteenth-century life, who had the potential to be immensely useful to a monarch seriously short of cash and still trying to figure out how to annul his marriage to his first wife and wed his mistress despite the opposition of at least half his subjects and most of Christendom. This heavy-set Londoner from Putney was a consummate problem solver, a crouching black panther with silken sinews and stealthy tread waiting to do its master's bidding. Smeaton bluntly asked him what he was doing at court and how he earned a living. 'You hold no royal office and possess no visible income. How do you manage, and how can I maintain the gentlemanly style we talked about before you miraculously found the cardinal's private papers?'

'I have not forgotten you,' Thomas laughed. 'Just give me time and you will be hunting in livery and dancing with a queen. I may hold no office but just yesterday, at the king's command, I was sworn into the Privy Council. Sir Thomas More, as Wolsey's successor to the Lord Chancellery, almost wet his pants at the thought of a potential heretic, who was once a friend of William Tyndale, sharing the responsibilities of government, and the Duke of Norfolk is sick to his stomach at the idea of sitting next to an ill-born commoner. But both men, like the king, find me useful, as did our former master. No matter the dignity of their titles they will always reward and promote a servant who can talk business with foreign wool merchants; knows by first name every criminal in London; speaks German, Latin, Italian, French and Spanish; and understands how Italian banking houses operate and European loans are negotiated, even if the fellow is a low-born varlet bleating a Putney patois and able to shoe a horse.'

'Well what exactly have you been doing for the last two months?'

'I have been talking to His Majesty about increasing his income, where to go to import the finest gossamer silks for his darling Anne Boleyn, how to build a topiary in the Italian style here in his privy garden, and which trees and bushes are best for pruning and shaping into mythological creatures. A dragon or a griffin would look well just over there close to that fountain. I have also been helping him remedy the scandal of Wolsey's two schools of learning at Ipswich and Oxford by closing them down. I did not, however, return their endowment to the plundered monasteries. The king's exchequer along with a few "deserving noblemen", if that is not a contradiction in terms, are the immediate beneficiaries. His Majesty is mightily pleased.'

'So that is the fate of the cardinal's pious efforts to build himself a high road to immortality: his contributions to higher learning with his coat of arms blazoned all over a boys' school at Ipswich, and scholars singing his praise at Cardinal College in Oxford, along with his unfinished work of art – his sepulchre with its marvellous stonework – were his prize monuments to history. The two centres of learning will cease to exist; his gorgeous coffin will never house his body. It's a pity. He was a great but flawed man who deserved better. Why don't you save his Oxford college and persuade His Majesty to give it his own name? You will have struck a blow for learning and flattered the king. Both worthy causes.'

'King's College, you mean? The best way to achieve that goal is to get Anne, who despite her haughty snobbery, favours education, to suggest the name to him. I will explain the price he will have to pay.'

Smeaton patted the older man on the back as if he were a friendly but anxious dog, which produced the awkward sight of a trim young man attempting to embrace a body sixty pounds heavier than himself. 'I hear nothing at court except complaints that now that Wolsey is dead nothing happens in government and that the King's Great Matter flounders in confusion. Now that you are on the Privy Council you must hear a bellyfull of ideas for satisfying His Majesty's marital needs.'

'I wish I had, but all we get are sighs and moans and ill temper. We sorely need a fresh start.'

Mark listened to the older man's complaints, then quietly said: 'Can't Parliament pass legislation?'

'I wish it could. It was called months ago to pass an Act of Attainder against Wolsey, but with the cardinal dead and gone to his doubtful reward, there has been nothing for it to do and has been adjourned until someone can come up with a plan.'

'Surely Parliament can act if it so desires. The king has tried to get an annulment of his marriage through papal law and failed. Why can't he get a divorce through parliamentary law?'

'On what grounds? State law cannot encroach on Church law.'

'Why not? Is the king inferior to the Pope in the eyes of God? Is English law inferior to Roman law? Did not parliamentary law outlaw papal interference in English Church affairs in the Statute of Praemunire back in the fourteenth century? Surely you can find someone who holds that parliamentary law is the highest law in the land, and can nullify any marriage if the Lords and Commons so decree and the king signs.'

'You know, Mark, the scowl that mars your musical brow is creased with dangerous but ingenious ideas, and I believe I know the man to talk to: Christopher St German, an aged but learned philosopher who can manufacture principles to fit any known facts faster than Cassandra could spin a prophesy, which, this time, will be believed as a new found article of faith for all the king's subjects. A statute made by the authority of the entire realm cannot be thought to recite a thing against the truth. As our old master predicted, Parliament can dry up papal revenues coming from England, and I see no reason why legislation can't be passed decreeing that all spiritual cases shall henceforth be adjudged within the king's jurisdiction and nowhere else. That should prevent Katherine from appealing her case to Rome and settle the annulment issue once and for all in the king's favour.'

Once started, Cromwell could not contain his enthusiasm. 'Yes, yes, you have set us on the right path. We will conjure up the Aristotelian principle that all political power is invested in and springs from the collective political community of the kingdom and expresses itself in parliamentary statutes as being the highest authority in the land, higher than any divine right claimed by the Pope. It is the voice of the people formulated by Parliament and translated into law by the king's signature. Crown and statute will decree Katherine's marriage to be unlawful and allow Henry to find himself a new wife. Well done, Mark!'

'But can you actually accomplish all of this, Thomas? Will Commons and Lords oblige and pass the necessary legislation? Will William Warham, the Archbishop of Canterbury, decrepit as he is, sanction such a divorce and remarriage? Will the kingdom welcome Anne as its new queen? She may be able to make the king's rod stand erect and tickle his mind with witty conversation and droll tales, but can she live down her reputation as an arrogant bitch and 'the devil of a concubine', as the Imperial ambassador refers to her?'

The king, back from trouncing Weston in two sets, ended Smeaton's questions before Cromwell could answer them. Both men rose and bowed, wishing His Majesty good day. Despite his victory at tennis the king was abrupt, and simply said, 'Smeaton, be in my closet at bedtime this evening.'

§

Henry was dressed in fur-lined slippers, a brocaded taffeta dressing gown trimmed in ermine and a tasselled nightcap. The weather had turned cold and a fire blazed in his bedroom, overpowering the light from a dozen candles. 'Oh, there you are, Mark. You didn't bring your lute, but never mind, try this one.' He picked up a six-string instrument with a bent-back peg box leaning against the wall, and said, 'It belonged to Giles Duwes, my old French teacher and magic lutenist. He died only a month ago and left me his lute. Here, take it and name a tune and I will accompany you.'

Mark admired Duwes' lute and began to play 'Pastime and Good Company', saying, 'I don't think we will need music scripts for this.'

Henry growled, 'Don't turn me into an octogenarian with bleary eyes and senile mind,' but he accompanied his rebuke with a smile. 'So you know my compositions.'

'Did you actually write "Greensleeves"?'

'Mostly yes and a little no. Giles Duwes introduced me to the new Italian style of composition and helped me compose the music. I wrote the lyrics obviously with the enchanting Anne Boleyn in mind; I was in the midst of courting her. Kings always get full credit.'

When the song was over Henry continued strumming chords on his lute, and finally asked, 'Mark, do you believe in dreams?'

'I am a singer and lutenist, Your Majesty, not a prophet.'

'True, but you do have dreams.'

'Yes, I dream of jousts and battles, coats of arms and finely wrought armour, masquerade dances and sumptuous feasts, ogres, witches, devils and beautiful women.'

'Do these scenes tell you anything, and do you believe them?'

'It all depends from whence they come. If they are the product of overly rich food and an upset stomach I am happy to awake and forget them as quickly as possible. If they are the result of worry, overwork and depression, I take them seriously but have a hard time remembering them in detail. If they are the words of the dead giving warning to the living, I go to confession and ask a priest. They say that God permits the dead to speak during the twelve days following Christmas.'

The king broke into Mark's discourse and said, 'My dream was three nights ago and about Wolsey offering my brother Arthur the papal crown. What do you think that is telling me? It seems extraordinarily unlikely. Can it have meaning?'

Mark picked up his lute and struck a few chords partly to delay answering, partly to give ambiance to his thoughts. 'The cardinal only died a little over a month ago; Prince Arthur, who lost his virginity to

Katherine of Aragon, has been much on your mind ever since you determined that your marriage to the queen was repugnant to both divine and human law; therefore it is not strange that they should dominate your dreams. Whether they are telling you something is another matter, but one possible meaning is that Wolsey is saying that as Lord Chancellor and Cardinal Legate he held the two highest offices in the realm, thereby combining all temporal and spiritual power in one person, himself, and he is saying you should do the same, be both pope and king. His crowning Arthur with a papal tiara is equally clear; kings of England are not only superior in the eyes of God to popes but also they should be their own popes in their own kingdoms. You will remember that the first King Arthur was deemed by the chronicler Geoffrey of Monmouth to be an emperor with powers stemming from the Roman emperor Constantine, who claimed dominion over Church and State. That is the message, as I interpret it, a sign to rethink your kingship and become an emperor, both king and pope in your own kingdom.'

As Henry listened to his lutenist the flame from the fire erupted into a flare, lighting the entire room and colouring the king's face a golden hue. The expression on his face changed imperceptibly from depressed thoughtfulness to joyous recognition, and he gave a little dance as he discerned the full implications of Mark's words. His lutenist had filled his dream world with new and wonderful ideas. A revolution of mind and spirit was in the making. 'You are an extraordinary man, Mark, wilful and daring; wasted on music. You should be on the Privy Council and direct its business.'

'Please Your Majesty, I am not prophesying the future, just suggesting one possible meaning of your dream. Remember I am only a songster.'

'Granted, but I think I like your interpretation; it has the ring of God's truth. Go to bed now, and let me meditate. Then I will summon Cromwell. It is never too late to discuss political theory with him.'

Smeaton smiled to himself and thought that Cromwell was a sufficiently flexible and astute man to successfully implement the king's dream of being Supreme Head of both State and Church of England. The king would decree his own divorce and that should bring Anne Boleyn to the marriage bed. Knowing Cromwell, he did not doubt that it would bring a great deal more than warm female flesh for His Majesty to enjoy. He shuddered; the poor man would have to gallop thirteen miles between London and Hampton Court Palace to reach His Majesty before dawn, a high price to pay for becoming the king's confidential advisor.

§

The bowlers were out in force this Friday morning; they were all members of the king's privy chamber – Henry Norris, Francis Weston, George Boleyn, William

Brereton and Thomas Wyatt – Henry VIII and Thomas Cromwell sat on the side line watching the play and refereeing the closeness of the bowls to the white jack. They were playing on the hilly green with bias balls to fit the contour of the land at Hampton Court Palace. The king had already laid down fifty crowns as a bet on Weston to win, and Cromwell was complaining that he could not afford such gambling sums.

'But this isn't gambling. This is a bet based on knowledge and experience. I know that young Weston is a master of the bowls and will win.'

'All the more reason for me to refuse the bet,' said Thomas. 'Moreover, I have news that will make you far richer and happier than winning a wager at bowls. Your personal supremacy of the Church of England has earned you £100,000!'

'Explain.'

'You will recall that Wolsey was on the verge of being attainted by Parliament for having violated the Statute of Praemunire. He died but he was not alone in his criminal activity. The entire Church of England collaborated and is equally guilty of violating parliamentary law. The Church in its southern and northern representative convocations have acknowledged their guilt and have begged for a pardon in return for a gift of £100,000. That, however, is only a trifle. The real power struggle began when your Privy Council demanded that the convocations also acknowledged you as "Sole Protector and Supreme Head of the English Church and clergy." This produced such a hue and cry that I settled for a compromise. The southern convocation has passed a submission of the clergy whereby it accepts you as supreme head "so far as the law of Christ allows."'

'That is not a compromise, that is total surrender,' roared the king, while at the same time managing to compliment Weston for a remarkably fine roll that placed his bowl inches away from the white jack.

'I know that patience is difficult when it involves something as complex and important as the royal supremacy. You know that I am not a betting man, but I will bet the same amount of money as you placed on Weston's win and wager that the qualification insisted by convocation on your supremacy will disappear as soon as Parliament passes the necessary legislation.'

'When will that be?'

'Soon, because first I shall write the law, and second because the political theory supporting the royal supremacy is already far advanced. You are head of the Church because God has made you so. It is an absolute and personal gift derived from heaven, descending downwards from God. At the same time, Parliament is in the process of authorising the same concept of royal supremacy as a power ascending upwards from the authority of the historic kingdom of England; the institutions which speak for the entire realm are king, lords and commons, in other words Parliament and its statutes.'

'I like what I hear, but what happens if my divinely inspired supremacy is questioned by Parliament's historically inspired supremacy. You have the making of a mighty conflict reducing the existing conflict with the papacy to chicken feed.'

Mercifully, before Cromwell could devise an answer, Weston won the bowling match and the king forgot to press the question in the midst of winning a handsome bet. Once a new match had started, His Majesty returned to the topic but not to the question. 'Tell me, Thomas, how goes our efforts to force Pope Clement into a more cooperative mood?'

'The Act of Annates is ready for your signature though, as you know, it had a difficult passage through both houses. It reduces to ninety-five per cent the traditional payment to the Pope of the first year's income by all newly installed bishops and high ecclesiastical officials, and redirects the monies to the royal exchequer. Your presence in Parliament assured its passage, but I doubt that it will achieve its purpose of impoverishing the papacy to the point that it will allow the annulment of your marriage. The law does not take effect for a year and you can enforce or cancel it at will. It is all bluff and Clement knows it. Far more important is the Act in Restraint of Appeals that is being written as we speak and changes the entire battle against Rome. Not only is Katherine's right to appeal her annulment trial to Rome proscribed but also Parliament for the first time has voiced what we were talking about just now, the theory of the royal supremacy, by calling England an empire beholden to nobody nor to any foreign law. Here, I have a copy of an early draft. Let me read it to you. "This realm of England is an empire, and so hath been accepted in the world, governed by one supreme head and king having the dignity and royal estate of the imperial crown." Parliament has bestowed an emperor's crown upon you!'

'I doubt whether it will feel any different from a normal crown, although probably heavier. It sounds impressive.' The king ran out of words, and spent the next few minutes inspecting the bowling game, where Weston was again winning. Turning again to Cromwell, he said: 'Changing the subject to a degree. What offices do you hold, Thomas?'

'None, Your Grace.'

'How would you like the Master of the Jewels and Clerk of the Hanaper; they pay well and require little work.'

'I am most grateful, Your Majesty, but I had hoped possibly for the Chancellor of the Exchequer. Your kingdom's finances need a strong hand.'

'You interest me but the exchequer must wait. The Jewels and Hanaper are yours immediately. We will speak tomorrow about my plans for Mistress Anne. I am hawking tomorrow morning and should be back by noon. Dine with me then. I will tell the dukes of Norfolk and Suffolk to join us.'

§

Cromwell was seated in one of the window alcoves shedding sunlight into one of the antechambers to the king's closet and bedroom. A banqueting table had been set for eight. The king's confidential adviser was covered with the grime of travel from an hour's horseback ride at a fast canter between London and Hampton Court. He wished the king had taken over York Place instead of turning it over to Anne Boleyn and her family as their London residence. It was now called Whitehall Palace and thousands of pounds were being spent to transform it from a residence fit for a cardinal into a mansion proper to a future queen. Henry had signed the Act in Restraint of Appeals, and even better, Archbishop Warham had conveniently died, making way for the forty-year-old Thomas Cranmer, an Oxford don, friend to Anne, and anxious to grant his sovereign an annulment from a wife defiantly determined to safeguard the regal succession of her daughter Mary. Nothing was left to be done except to ennoble the Lady Boleyn and make her suitable for marriage to a king, and introduce her to his brother sovereign, François of France. Henry had finally decided to go it alone, and get an annulment without papal blessings.

Henry had arrived back at Hampton Court an hour earlier, his clothes covered with black muck and his mouth full of mud. He had been carried back in the falconer's wagon filled with caged birds. His favourite gyr falcon, appropriately the sovereign of all birds of prey, had attacked a pheasant but the falcon had dropped its victim in mid-air. Anxious to reach his quarry before it could take wing and escape, Henry had used his jumping stick to hop from hummock to hummock to avoid the brackish waters of the wetland into which the bird had fallen. The king's staff broke in the midst of a mighty leap, he had fallen, stunned and face down in the muddy water. Had not Francis Weston been close behind the king might have smothered. Weston pulled his sovereign into a sitting position and called for the falconer's wagon to cart the king, still gasping for breath, home. By the time Cromwell arrived Henry was well scrubbed, his mouth washed out with a fine German white wine, and his clothes sent to the laundry. It had been a most undignified and unkingly experience for a monarch who prided himself on his athletic ability, and he chose to forget the entire embarrassing episode.

He arrived in his private dining room not exactly with fanfare but strumming on a lute and singing:

> 'Thomas Cromwell was a crafty sod
> Who committed cunning deeds.
> In recompense he ate the king's bread
> And drank two mugs of mead.'

'Not one of my better rhymes but sufficient to greet a blacksmith-brewer, loan shark and lawyer at mealtime on a sunny winter day. The Privy Council is getting used to your Putney accent which appears only when you speak English; Anne says your French is near perfect. You may manage my household but you lack sufficient hereditary status to handle State policy and control my kingdom. Come, let us start eating. I am ravenous.' He sat in the only armchair available, picked up the flagon of wine and poured himself and Cromwell generous drinks into their ornate crystal beakers. Cromwell gladly accepted the drink in hopes of lessening the sting of the king's insult to his social status.

'If Norfolk and Suffolk and their famished advisors are late for food, they can go without. So tell me Cromwell, what am I going to do about the adorable but infuriating Mistress Boleyn and her grasping relatives?'

Cromwell had been told about the king's hunting accident but sensed that it was not a subject for table conversation. Instead he simply mumbled, 'I hope Your Majesty is feeling well?'

'There is nothing wrong with me but a little mud on my face which has now been washed away. Now, about Anne; how much is a marchioness worth? Ah, here comes the food.' As Henry spoke a large roast of beef was being carved. 'Do you know what these strange looking utensils are?' He picked up what looked like a miniature trident by his plate. 'You no longer have to spear your meat with a knife; you use this fork that doubles for a spoon to scoop the food so long as it is not liquid. They are newly arrived from France. Mighty inventive, these Frenchies.'

Thomas knew about forks but in fact had never used one. Watching the king carefully, he imitated him, and said, 'A marchioness, created in her own rights, is worth whatever your exchequer can afford.'

'And how much is that. I am scarcely expected to know how much I am worth. Let's say £2,000 a year.'

'Your treasurer might complain.'

'Let's be as tight as Midas and say £1,000.'

'I think your exchequer could handle that and keep the Lady Anne uncomplaining.'

'Agreed. She complains far too much. We can use Welsh manors for the bulk of her income. That will deprive no one of importance. We will entitle her Marchioness of Pembroke, a sound Welsh name. Well that is completed; we have Anne's financial future settled, and here come Norfolk and Suffolk and their league of hungry retainers. I do wish they would tell my master server how many people he is expected to feed.'

By the time the dukes were seated and their followers scattered about the room, the second course of meat pie was being served and the meal concluded with custard for dessert.

Henry brought his dukes up to date: 'I have been arranging with Master Cromwell to ennoble Anne with an endowment of £1,000 a year. He will arrange the ceremony, and I want both of you in attendance. The full court will be on display and its best behaviour. I want her ennoblement to be a magnificent affair, a way of introducing her to the kingdom and endowing her with sufficient dignity so that I can have her meet François I as my future bride. Suffolk, will it do any good to invite my sister, your wife?'

'No, my lord, she is a sick woman and very stubborn.'

Henry added under his breath, 'and she detests Anne Boleyn. I have never understood why.' Out loud, he said to Cromwell, 'The ceremony will take place at Windsor Castle and will be on Sunday the first of September. Anne's Norfolk cousin, Mary Howard, bride to my son Henry Fitzroy, can carry the gold coronet of a marchioness. I shall order the Lady Katherine to return her crown jewels; that will please Anne no end. We can leave what to wear to the lady herself; she possesses an impeccable sense of style. I myself will bestow her patent of nobility and grant her lands sufficient to maintain her new rank in society.'

§

Crossing the English Channel is rarely a pleasant or tranquil experience, and the 2,000 noblemen and gentlemen who accompanied Henry VIII and Anne in their journey to meet the King of France gave a collective sigh of relief, settled their queasy stomachs and put away their images of Saint Christopher, the patron saint of safe travel, when the port of Calais came into view. Cromwell sailed in the king's vessel, the *Swallow*; so did Mark Smeaton, for Henry liked to play the lute whenever the sea grew rough and required him as accompaniment. Mark was not convinced that music eased *mal de mer* but he did as he was ordered.

Cromwell had financial duties to attend. The cost of entertaining François at Calais was estimated at £6,000 and vastly more would be spent if the king actually wedded his newly created marchioness. He needed at least £50,000 in cash, and Cromwell's primary task was to borrow the money on the European money market. Since the purpose of the trip was to impress the French king and his kingdom with the splendour of Henry's possible bride, song and music were essential, and Mark Smeaton was just as busy as his friend Cromwell. From dawn to midnight singing, dancing and the sound of music beset the atmosphere, and many of the French king's retinue remembered with delight Smeaton when he had travelled with Cardinal Wolsey singing his way through France back in 1529.

The English king and his gorgeously attired marchioness were greeted by the thunderous sound of a royal salute and a magnificent reception given by the mayor and lord deputy of England's last bit of land in France. Royal and religious protocol had been finely attuned. The French king would arrive without his second wife, who could not be invited because she was Katherine of Aragon's niece and disapproved of Anne. Nor could François spend too much time with Anne without unsettling the Pope, so it was arranged that Henry would visit François in the neighbouring French town of Bologne for a four-day 'stag party', and François would accompany him back to Calais for a formal introduction to Anne. This required playing down the female side of the reception, and Anne was escorted by only the female members of her family and friends. She made a dramatic entrance, dressed in an exotic golden robe with see-through slashes to reveal a silver gown beneath, her face masked and her dancing partner the French king.

Anne had been upset by the limits set on the lavishness and expense of the clothes worn by the aristocracy of both kingdoms, but not even her critical eye could detect any outward signs of disrespect to the hopeful bride. Nothing could equal the 3,000-gun salute that greeted the French monarch or the £3,500 diamond he bestowed on Anne. Even the sun shined for his four days in Calais, turning the October days into a sumptuous display of late summer which François spent dancing, banqueting and chatting with the newly ennobled French-speaking marchioness to the point that Henry was made ridiculously jealous by the sight of such friendship. He was only satisfied when Anne was safely away from French banter, housed in the Calais Exchequer, a palace-like building with its own tennis court, private gardens for both Henry and Anne, a great gallery replete with pictures of kings and emperors from times out of memory, and a seven-room suite for Anne with a bedroom backing up on to Henry's own sleeping quarters, with a locked interconnecting door.

Henry stood in front of the fire attired in a nightshirt that bunched around his neck forming a ruffle and hanging voluminously in folds from his shoulders to the floor, revealing surprising small and delicate feet.

Little wonder the king had fallen on his face chasing after a wounded pheasant. François of France had departed in a final blast of musical farewells, and so had the sunshine, to be replaced by a villainous north-western storm, making the channel waves so high that Henry thought Poseidon and Zeus must have joined forces to wipe the waters of all shipping. The more daring members of his party had ventured out into the wind and rain, only to be washed ashore on the Burgundian-Flemish coast. His own vessel had not run the risk of heavy seas and had scurried back into port to outwait the weather.

As the king warmed his bottom in front of the flames, and meditated the sad passage of time, he remembered a day when he was twenty-one and willing to defy ocean waves in a small boat, but now at forty-one he confessed he was more interested in personal safety and the welfare of his future wife. They were housed together with a locked door between them, waiting for the weather to change. Suddenly the door joining their suites opened without a sound, and Anne stood in the doorway, hair down and covering her back, dressed in a light nightgown.

'I thought that door was locked,' the king exclaimed.

Without a word, Anne ran across the room, leaned down and picked up the hem of his nightshirt and lifted it as high as his crotch. She then let go and grabbed his privy parts with both hands and began to knead and squeeze his equipment. She laughed at the surprised and expectant smile that appeared on his face, and could feel his whole body as well as his penis grow rigid. Henry turned to the far end of the room where Sir Henry Norris, his groom of the stool, stood in the shadows, and said: 'Get your ass out of here, Norris, and don't try leaving by Lady Pembroke's door.' When Norris had departed, Anne continued her fondling, saying: 'No more chastity and abstinence for us. We may not have the Pope's blessings but we most certainly have the King of France's. He told me, and I think he said the same to you, that we should go it alone and let the Pope and emperor threaten what they will, which will be all threats and no action.'

'He said the same to me but in more exalted terms. Come drag me to bed by any means you choose.' As Anne guided him to bed with both hands still locked between his legs, she gave him a kiss and said, 'The timing is perfect, my body is ready and I shall forge you a wonderful heir to the throne.'

'Let go of the royal jewels, get on the bed and let me take my pleasure. I am ready to flood you with royal sperm. It would be a terrible crime to cast my seed on the ground, so kindly let go of my testicles.'

'Henry, you are such a prude! No one ever refers to his balls as testicles except you. It sounds so medical.'

As Anne manoeuvred the king into bed she found herself still thinking about her lover's prudery, and she remembered an occasion when they were floating down the river to Greenwich Palace where she had rooms, and Henry challenged one of his gentlemen to a rhyming contest. As they approached the palace he burst into poetry:

> 'Within this tower
> There lieth a flower
> That hath my heart.'

His rival composer countered with:

> 'Within this hour
> She pist full sower
> And let a fart.'

Anne laughed at the words, but the king was not amused and bid his gentleman 'Avant varlet, begone.' Anne smiled at the memory that rapidly disappeared into the enjoyment of sex.

Anne awoke in her great four-poster bed with the bed curtains firmly closed, shutting out all light. It was early December and cold. Her blankets were tucked firmly around her neck, and a marvellous sense of satisfaction pervaded her entire body. She wondered at the source of such contentment. Puzzling over the problem, she asked herself if it was because she was sleeping for the first time in Cardinal Wolsey's old palace of York Place, now called Whitehall Palace. New quarters fit for a queen had been added and the entire building renovated. All this had been done by a besotted royal lover who would do anything to please her, for when they were in Calais last October meeting the French sovereign, Henry had spoken of marriage. She nestled deeper under the covers enjoying the warmth and thinking that her sensation of wellbeing stemmed from something more than palatial housing enhanced by the knowledge that Wolsey was knocking at the walls of his grave in agitation at the thought of a woman he had called a strumpet and 'the midnight crow' owning his magnificent residence. No, her feeling of delectation was something more visceral than pleasant housing. It was positively biological, and she pulled back her bed curtains and called for her minions who regularly waited on her.

Two ladies were already sitting in her bedchamber and a third appeared at the door. Anne always thought of them as her three furies or fates, each personifying an aspect of her own character. They were all faithful friends who Anne did not hesitate to badger and make the butt of her own ill temper. Her sister Mary Boleyn was soft, fair and cuddlesome, and forever satisfying men attracted by her sensuous hips crying out for penetration and breasts ripe for fondling. Her sexual appeal was so great that men were transported to acts of folly and rape. She had been a dazzling sexual success when she and Anne were for a short time in Paris as teenagers, acquiring a worldwide renowned for her permissiveness. She had been easily enticed into

Henry VIII's bed, and had been promptly married off to William Carey of the king's privy chamber when her belly began to swell with child. There would be no recognition for this baby as a royal bastard as had been conferred on Henry's first illegitimate child, Henry Fitzroy, even though the Carey infant had been christened Henry too. Anne was just as pleased; she did not want two bastards interfering with the succession. William Carey died of the sweating sickness in 1528 and ever since, Mary had been a forlorn but still extremely attractive dependent of her far more vivacious and ambitious sister. Anne regarded her as the Venus of the Boleyn family and useful as a possible midwife. She sat on a three-legged stool close to Anne's bed, embroidering the Marchioness of Pembroke's new coat of arms on her sister's clothing.

Beside Mary, on an equally uncomfortable stool, sat Elizabeth Browne, the Countess of Worcester, a lady of endless enthusiasm but little common sense. Cherub faced and wide eyed, she loved to hunt and game and often out-sported the men. She was sitting now with a lute in her lap, quietly playing chords and humming to herself. Anne always fancied her as Artemis, the goddess of the hunt – shoot first, ask questions later – but a devoted and useful friend. At the door stood Jane Parker, Lady Rochford, the wife of Anne's brother, George Viscount Rochford. She was as sharp, angular, and cold as Mary Boleyn was soft, fair and cuddly; as intelligent and cynical as Lady Worcester was enthusiastic and boisterous.

Anne suspected that she would be at home on the Greek island of Lesbos for she detested her husband and was cool to all male approaches. If she belonged to Anne's imaginary pantheon of goddesses she was closest to Hecate, the goddess of magic, witchcraft and necromancy.

Anne ordered her three furies to her bedside and asked, 'Why do I feel so gladdened this morning? I am positive that life is worth living despite the pessimistic creed of our Church that claims that death is more important than life.'

Elizabeth Browne answered that she was certain that Anne's attitude foretold a good day at the hunt; her falcon would catch a pheasant and they would all eat well that night. Jane said in her usual throaty voice, 'Because your gladdened soul is remembering that Wolsey's unpleasant spirit remains trapped in its grave and no one hears or cares about his helpless knocking to get out and haunt the living.'

Mary asked, 'Have you had any physical disturbances lately?'

Anne thought back and finally said: 'Well yesterday I burped my head off and this morning my breasts are tingling, and I twice had to use the chamber pot.'

Mary reached up and kissed her sister. 'You know what I think. I think you are pregnant with the king's heir to the throne!'

Anne was silent as she digested this suggestion. Then she exclaimed, 'Oh, my god, I know you are right! I am indeed pregnant! You may all leave the room and let me talk to my newly conceived child who needs all the love and comforting he can get as a Tudor child.' Anne pulled the covers back over her and began to reminisce. She recalled with a smile a scene when she had been dining with both Henry and Katherine and the royal couple had indulged in a first-class row in which Katherine had accused her husband of neglect and cruelty, Henry had countered by calling the Pope a heretic. His queen had laughed in his face at the thought, and the king had walked out of the room in a huff. Anne remembered later taxing her lover and shouting at him, 'Did I not tell you that whenever you dispute with the queen she was sure to have the upper hand? I see that some fine morning you will succumb to her reasoning and that you will cast me off, and that will be the end of the war with Rome. I have been waiting long and might in the meanwhile have contracted some advantageous marriage, out of which I might have had issue, which is the greatest consolation in this world. But, alas! Farewell to my time and youth spent to no purpose at all.'

She had been furious then but now the shoe was on the other foot, she had issue, and Henry, despite his hankering for a papal annulment of his marriage, would have to marry her immediately! Her time and youth were no longer being spent to no purpose. That would shut the old queen up, and she would have to be satisfied with the title Dowager Princess of Wales and her daughter, deprived of her princess status, was now only the Lady Mary. Anne had never forgiven the queen when, as a gift to the king, she was requested to give up her jewellery so that Anne could be properly bedecked when elevated to the nobility as Marchioness of Pembroke. Katherine had rudely refused, claiming it would be a deadly sin to allow them to adorn 'the scandal of Christendom'. Henry had to write and command her to obey his orders. 'What a bitch she was!' Anne thought. It was wonderful to think that Katherine and her worthless daughter would soon be outranked and forgotten. She recited to herself the mantra, 'I will be crowned queen.'

Anne settled back to enjoy this thought when suddenly another idea popped into her head. 'I will be not only a queen but also a mother.' And with that idea rising like a tide in her head, she suddenly realised that everything had changed. She had started at court merely determined to become a political force; she had risen from commoner to marchioness with her own coat of arms; reaching out for the crown now seemed entirely possible. She lay back and dreamed of becoming a queen. But now something far grander was looming; a tiny ember of creation in her womb was calling out for protection. Her primary goal in life was no longer political and social success but the preservation of this small spark of life she was harbouring; her purpose was to plant her seed on the political history of the kingdom and prepare for a Boleyn royal inheritance. As a mother of a king, all things were possible!

As Anne cuddled in bed with her happy dreams, another thought came to her, and she rang loudly for her ladies in waiting. Elizabeth Browne appeared at the door. 'Elizabeth, my dear, order me nine yards of gold cloth and arrange for a fitting for a new gown with matching bodice and blouse. The collar should be high necked to display my most dominant feature and the bodice covered with pearls. If there is any material left over, have the tailor make me a small cloak and stop him from substituting sequins for real pearls. I need a new dress in which to tell Henry that he is at last a father!'

Mark Smeaton rose quietly at four in the morning; he slept in a bed and room shared by two other singers. No stars could be seen in the cold and cloudy skies of a January day in 1533. He had been ordered by Henry Norris, the groom of the stool and chief of the king's privy chamber, to come in absolute secrecy to the newly constructed Cockpit Gate, sometimes called the Holbein Gate. How Holbein, a common artist, got his name attached, he did not know. It was so new its walls had just been painted and the great gallery with its immense bay and double tier of four windows overlooking the tilting yard had only been furnished with a few chairs and tables. Norris had whispered to him that the king had wanted him at his wedding but no one had said in what capacity – guest or performer. He dressed hurriedly but warmly, and to be on the safe side grabbed his lute before walking across the Preaching Place to Cockpit Gate.

There he found that Norris and the king had preceded him and were waiting in one of the two small chambers on each side of the gallery; it would not do that the groom meet the bride before the marriage ceremony. The guests, or more accurately the witnesses, were waiting in the great gallery and were only a handful in number – Thomas Heneage and William Brereton of the king's privy chamber and Mary Boleyn and Lady Worcester waiting upon Anne. Rowland Lee, a staunch supporter of the king's annulment to Katherine and later Bishop of Lichfield, was the spiritual celebrant for the occasion. Since secrecy was paramount – the royal nominee for archbishop, Thomas Cranmer, had not yet been confirmed by the Pope, who at all costs must not be stampeded into refusing to sanctify the appointment by discovering that Henry had already defied him – the hour assigned, the small number of witnesses involved, and the unlikely location all made excellent sense. Mark wondered whether the ceremony itself would be truncated so as to get the participants back to the palace before dawn and the palace's awakening. He was quite sure there would be no high mass or wedding feast, and noticed that there were no flowers or singing boys.

Anne arrived last, attired in an everyday dress, her third best, but garlanded with a crown of rosemary on her head and her hair hanging abundantly around her shoulders. Henry likewise was dressed in normal clothing sans jewellery or the symbols of monarchy, and his fingers were bare of rings and ornaments. Lee started the ceremony in the traditional fashion, asking whether anyone knew cause why Anne and Henry should not be married. He then asked the king whether he had 'the Pope's licence'. Henry was prepared for the question and answered 'Yes'. What he meant was he had the pontiff's dispensation, written years before, to marry, not Anne per se, but 'the sister of someone with whom he had had illicit sex' – i.e. Mary Boleyn. Rowland Lee pressed further and asked to see the disposition. The king, using his full magisterial voice, answered in considerable irritation: 'Think you me a man of so small and slender foresight and consideration of my affairs that unless all things were safe and sure would enterprise this matter? I have truly a licence ... which if it were seen, should discharge us all.' No one at this hour of the morning could expect him to go and get it. Unwilling to call his sovereign a liar, Lee proceeded with the oft-spoken words of matrimony.

To the question whether Henry would take Anne as his wife, the king answered: 'I take thee Anne as my wedded wife, to have and to hold, from this day forward, for better, for worse, for richer, for poorer, in sickness and in health, till death us do part, if holy Church it will ordain, and thereto I plight thee my troth.' Anne then answered, repeating the same oath but adding to her promise 'to be bonny and buxom in bed and at board.' Lee then placed the ring that Norris gave him on Anne's thumb, saying 'In the name of the father,' he moved the ring to her index finger and said 'In the name of the son,' and finally placed the ring on her fourth finger of her right hand saying 'In the name of the holy spirit, with this ring I thee wed.'

All this time Mark had been a bystander but after Rowland Lee's pronouncement he picked up his lute and burst into a few verses of Greensleeves as the company moved out of the gallery and back to the palace:

> I have been ready at your hand,
> To grant whatever you would crave,
> I have both wagered life and land,
> Your love and good will for to have.
> Greensleeves was all my joy
> Greensleeves was my delight,
> Greensleeves was my heart of gold,
> And who but my Lady Greensleeves.

Mark hurried after the newlyweds and their attendants, wondering whether they all would be fed a wedding breakfast. He was hungry and hoped so. He followed the group to the palace and into the king's private dining hall, where everyone seated themselves but left a single empty place to the left of the bride. Mark guessed that there was confusion over the protocol of whether to sit next to a king's wife and the guests had resolved the problem by leaving the place empty. When Anne spotted Mark still standing, she called out 'Here comes the musician with the exquisite voice and magic fingers, come sit down next to me, it is the only seat left, and it has been a long time since we had an intimate conversation.'

'Yes,' thought Smeaton, 'not since you insulted my voice and manhood five years ago.' He no longer hated Anne and still felt her sex appeal but ever since he arrived at court he was never comfortable in her presence. He could not say that he really liked the new queen.

It was barely light outside and the winter sun had not yet risen. The room was lit by candles but was still dark in the corners where servants clustered to serve the king and his company. Despite the early hour, it was clear that none of them realised that His Majesty had just been married. Anne's interest in Mark Smeaton was interrupted briefly by a question put to her by the king, but soon she gave him her full attention. 'Mark,' she said, 'now that I will soon be setting up my own household, why don't you and your sultry voice leave the king's service and join my chambers and play lute and virginal and sing for me? I can give you a private bedchamber. I am sure I can arrange the exchange with Henry.'

Mark was tempted; his bedfellows snored and he sensed that Anne's chambers, filled with pretty young ladies in waiting, would be far more exciting than the king's all-male privy chamber. He cautiously answered, 'If you can afford me, my lady, I would be delighted.'

Anne replied with a touch of haughtiness in her words: 'Of course I can afford you; I will be queen.'

§

March was a month heavy with historic events. The papal bull ratifying and sanctifying Thomas Cranmer's appointment as archbishop arrived. The Appeals Statute, not only referring to England as an empire but also preventing Katherine from appealing her case to Rome, passed both houses of parliament. Convocation pronounced in the king's favour on the annulment of his marriage to his wife, and four days later Thomas Cranmer was consecrated Archbishop of Canterbury. On the day before Easter, Anne went to church glittering in jewels and a golden gown, and publicly received full regal recognition. It was clearly time to call in Thomas Cromwell and his managerial talents and prepare for Anne Boleyn's coronation as Queen of England. He only had two months to make ready the most lavish celebration in centuries. The king was explicit, he demanded pageants and tableaux, symbols and displays to exalt the divine nature of the Tudor monarchy and God's applause for Henry's new queen, whose growing belly was clearly the saviour of his dynasty and the kingdom. Money was of no concern but time was of the essence; the king demanded that his queen be crowned on Sunday the first of June when the flowers would be in full bloom and his dynasty at its height. That the crowning was to be followed by high mass and a magnificent banquet for 800 guests that together would take nine hours to perform was in no way regarded as overtaxing to the six-month pregnant queen.

Cromwell grumbled to himself, 'Two months to perform a miracle'; he had indeed become indispensable to the king. His first job, he thought, was to get in touch with his old friend and incomparable painter Hans Holbein for artistic designs and ideas. (He had met Holbein when both men worked for Wolsey back in 1526–7.) After that he would go to the lord mayor of the city and beg or bribe him to persuade the city's livery companies to put on public displays and performances, not to mention commandeer their water barges to transport Anne and the entire court from Greenwich Palace to the Tower of London where the grand procession would begin. The schedule called for some fifty barges, each at least sixty feet long with covered cabins and oared by eight rowers on each side, all adorned with gold foil and paint and led by a fire spewing dragon on a small wherry in front of the barges that signalled a salute of cannon fire from every ship they passed. Every barge carried singers and musicians to herald both God and man of the arrival of a new queen. They were to be accompanied by a flotilla of 200 lesser vessels carrying the entire court up the river and across to the Tower. On Saturday an immense parade of privy councillors, government officials, and peers and peeresses of the realm would march with Anne in a gorgeous litter through the city, past Saint Paul's Cathedral to the Strand and hence on to Westminster Palace and the Abbey where Anne would be crowned queen. The event would be the talk of the kingdom.

The following Monday morning Anne, Cromwell, Smeaton, Jane Parker and Lady Worcester were all gathered in the queen's gallery at Whitehall Palace reliving the exploits and wonders of the past weekend. 'I don't understand,' said Lady Worcester, 'I never laid eyes on the king during the parade, coronation or banquet. Was he ill?'

'No,' said Cromwell, 'that's tradition. Kings are never seen at their queen's crowning. Henry had his own private viewing space at both the crowning and the banquet. He had an excellent view.'

'I was amazed and delighted that my white falcon had such an important part to play in the performance,' interrupted Anne. 'He appeared first, far larger than life size, on a rowboat beside my barge. Surrounded by red and white roses and sitting on a golden tree stump on a green hill that sported a cluster of virgins singing and playing lutes. He had a crown on his head and a sceptre under his wing. I thought the scene exquisitely sweet and the message wonderfully to the point. You, Mark, weren't there dressed as a virgin. Were you?'

'Certainly not, Your Highness, I was with the king, my lute in hand.' He turned to Cromwell and asked: 'Which tableaux display did you like best?'

'There is no debate. It was the castle-like structure that I had built on Gracechuch Street with a cupola on the roof and the floor painted green and undulating like a meadow. There a tree stump was constructed bursting with red and white roses like the scene on the wherry by Your Highness's barge. On the green floor sat Saint Anne, your patron saint, and her entire family, including a child, greeted your litter as it passed and spoke words of hope that you would someday rival the maternal successes of your patron saint.' He recited,

> 'Right so, dear Queen most excellent!
> Highly endured with all gifts of grace,
> As by your living is well apparent;
> We the citizens, by you in short space
> Hope such issue and descent to purchase;
> Wherein the same faith shall be defended,
> And this City from all dangers preserved.

'I remember the lines well because my friend Nicholas Udall wrote them and I helped. You will recall that as soon as the young boy had spoken, a painted cloud in the ceiling opened up and a white falcon flew down and nestled among the flowers and an angel descended to place an imperial crown on the bird's head. Finally another younger voice proclaimed,

> "To crown with a diadem imperial
> In her honour rejoice we all,
> For it cometh from God, and not of man
> Honour and grace be to our Queen Anne!"'

'There must have been 200 children singing and reciting,' commented Lady Worcester. 'I thought their voices and performances lovely. It made the pageantry seem real and human. Someone help out my memory and bad education, and tell me, how did Saint Anne come to be a saint?'

'Idiot,' answered the new queen. 'She was the Virgin Mary's mother and founder of the holy family. That should be enough to make anybody a saint. What I want to know is whether anyone saw Sir Thomas More in the parade?' The silence was deafening. Anne responded to the silence in a bitter voice, 'That man is the all-time traitor, posing as a loyal subject of the king but in fact undermining his supremacy and authority, and secretly working for the Pope. He is the most detestable man I know and I don't understand why Henry puts up with him. He is at the top of my list of traitors who must be eliminated.'

Mark suddenly broke in – he liked Sir Thomas and was uncomfortable at the queen's tirade – and announced that he had liked best the classical theme, especially the tableaux depicting the Judgment of Paris in which Paris is given a golden apple by Jupiter to present to the fairest goddess of them all – Juno, Athene, or Venus. The ladies wagered for the prize, and Paris awarded it to Venus. At this point a fourth lady appears and a child's voice speaks:

'Here is the fourth lady now in our presence
Most worthy to have it, of due congruence,
As peerless in riches, wit and beauty,
Which are but sundry qualities in you three.
But for her worthiness, this apple of gold
Is too simple a reward, a thousand fold.'

'You all remember, another child then presented Anne with the crown imperial, to show that she is the harbinger of a new and golden age, and a choir of men and boys serenaded their queen. I thought the song and music throughout the procession was magnificent.'

Jane finally spoke up, 'Your Highness, allow me to inquire why I was not asked to attend at your table during the banquet. Lady Worcester was there helping to hold the sheet that hid you when you needed to spit or blow your nose. I should have been at the other end of the curtain, but you asked the Countess of Oxford instead. Given all I have done for you, the least you could have done was to allow me to be one of the two ladies beneath your table waiting to do your bidding. You forget that it was my due as a member of the Boleyn family. Moreover, my usefulness to you goes back a long way.'

Anne took a long time to answer, staring steadily at her lady in waiting. 'Jane, it was the most joyous day of my life and I wanted only happy people around me. You are not nor ever have been a happy person. You detest your husband, my brother, and you rarely have a pleasant thing to say about anybody. I accept all this because you are versed in the occult and useful to have around. An abhorrent husband, whom I find a thoughtful and congenial brother, is no basis for claiming family status in the Boleyn clan. You rode in my retinue behind my litter and I think that the proper place for you. It is time for all of us to leave and find something to eat.'

Nobody heard her but Jane got the last word in before leaving the room: 'Just remember, my lady, it is always dangerous to insult even a devil's disciple. Your never know when Satan might be listening.'

§

Mark Smeaton stood at a far-distant corner of Whitehall Palace's freshly mowed southern lawn. He was enjoying the perfect painter's composition of the verdant green of immaculately cut grass, the blueness of a cloudless sky, the freshness of an early September day, and the riot of colour from the queen's ladies standing or sitting on the grass dressed in gorgeous colourful court attire and clustered about an upholstered chair where Her Highness, the queen, sat in lonely splendour. No man was permitted anywhere near the pregnant queen. For the past three weeks the queen had retired into confinement, where no man was allowed.

Smeaton wondered why painters never depicted such a perfect display of colours. They painted cows munching in their meadows, peasants labouring in their fields, swans swimming in their rivers but never ladies in all their glory. The scene was bright with exotic colours, filled with latent drama and overflowing with catty gossip, everything a painter needed. Yet no professional artist responded. Was it because such views were regarded as an invasion of privacy? Yet ladies loved to have their portraits painted, the more flamboyant and multicoloured their clothing the better. Some day, Mark thought, artists would give up dreary religious subjects and concentrate on life as it was actually lived.

As Smeaton watched the ever-changing whorl of clashing hues as satins and silks sparkled in the sunlight, he wondered what the focal point of this resplendent composition was thinking as she sat expressionless watching her ladies frolicking before her: probably about the future prince who was scheduled to arrive in a day or two. Anne was indeed thinking about her future son, but not as Smeaton envisaged. She was tired of being pregnant and ignored by her husband. She enviously regarded her ladies' trim figures and compared them to what she felt was her own deformed shape; she thought of it as a hideous goitre-like bulge protruding out in front. God, she thought, had been unnecessarily harsh on the mother of mankind when he inflicted the pain of childbirth, and worse, the indignity of nine months of pregnancy, as punishment for tempting silly Adam to eat of the apple of knowledge.

Anne's child arrived on schedule – the seventh of September. For the past fifteen days, a room had been sealed off from masculine contamination; its walls and ceiling and all but one window hung with tapestries to block out the light and dangerous fresh air. Anne retired into the midst of feminine wisdom and ancient folklore, surrounded by her ladies, to remerge with a baby in her arms to present to her husband and monarch. Except Anne could not get herself to complete the ritual; her child was not the son confidently foretold by astrologers, physicians, witches and wizards, but a girl, worthless to the king and his succession, and worthless to Anne in maintaining her supremacy at court. The disappointment was too great; she remained in bed and let Jane Rochford, who had an unusually happy smile on her face, carry the infant out of the birthing chamber. The name Elizabeth, after Henry's mother, had been preselected months ago in the unlikely case of a female child.

All Anne wanted was to be left alone to meditate on the unfairness and precariousness of life. God had given her a child but of the wrong sex. She sensed the stealth of the devil in ruining what should have been her day of greatest triumph. Her ladies kept bothering her. 'Wouldn't you like to see your baby and cuddle her?' they asked. Anne sighed and thought, 'I must act the expected role of loving mother even though I feel like a prisoner expecting to be pardoned and freed but told that she was going to be immediately executed.'

'Your Highness,' said her sister, Mary, 'You must give thought to the baby's future, her household, where it will be located and its staffing. Who will be in charge? Then you must decide on where, when and under what circumstances you plan to see her. Do you plan to wean her yourself or must a wet nurse be found? Do you want regulated visiting hours by the day or by the week?'

'Go away, Mary, and leave me to my sorrows for a few hours. I will soon be back in control; I will speak to Henry and assure him that the baby Elizabeth augurs lots of future healthy children, all male, and I will be a proper mother. I am a superb actress.'

With her attendants gone, she lay quietly in bed imagining her yet to be born son in her arms. The image kept changing and dissolving: first a young boy, then a squealing girl and finally a crowned falcon with a sceptre under its wing.

CHAPTER IV

The War Against the Monks and Friars

Henry was sitting in one of his withdrawing rooms eating breakfast of a chicken stew washed down by a light Flemish ale when Thomas Cromwell knocked on the door and was told to enter. 'And what hat are you wearing this morning Master Cromwell?' inquired the king.

'Since I am here at your command at this early hour, I am wearing all four of them – Master of the Jewels, Principal Secretary, Chancellor of the Exchequer and Master of the Rolls. What is your desire, Your Majesty, this day?'

'I have been thinking, which is always a dangerous pastime. Would you call me a great king compared to foreign sovereigns and historic English monarchs?'

Cromwell knew from past experience that the hardest part of being Henry VIII's confidential adviser was answering his more philosophical questions, most of which were like 'Why do the sun and stars exist?' A little flattery always helped. 'My job, Sire, is to make you the greatest sovereign on earth. Always remember Erasmus's words of praise: "This king possesses a lively mentality which reaches the stars, and he is able beyond measure to bring to perfection whatever task he undertakes. He attempts nothing which he did not bring to a successful conclusion.'"

'Then you have failed miserably in fulfilling all your hats. I am no William the Conqueror, no Henry II, a great administrator and empire builder, no Edward I, a magnificent warrior. Compared to the Emperor Charles and François I of France I am miniscule. They have kingdoms twice to three times the population of England. François' parliaments are pussycats compared to my tigerish parliaments which begrudge every extra penny in taxes I request and my kingdom is known for its civil wars and feudal unrest. Charles is the military Leviathan of Europe. If it were not for the fourth player in the arena of kings, Suleiman the Magnificent of the Ottoman empire, who regularly knocks on the doors of Vienna threatening to turn it into yet another Islamic city, and as we speak is making his military presence known on the high seas in the Mediterranean and in Tunisia, Charles would have long since disciplined his German Lutheran princes, exterminated Martin Luther's vile heresy, and very likely invaded England to replace me with his niece, Katherine of Aragon. No, I am not even a third-rate player in European affairs, and Cardinal Wolsey in his prime had an income equal to my own. Kings of England are not even wealthier than their own subjects. What are you going to do about it?'

'How serious are you in painting yourself such an inferior monarch?'

'Very! Why do you think I appointed you Chancellor of the Exchequer at your own request? Why do you think I made you, a commoner and blacksmith's son, Principal Secretary – to help me shoe my hunting steeds? Cromwell, I want ideas, I want action, I want money. I need to get things done.'

'Fortunately for both of us, I have a number of monetary notions.'

'Excellent! State them.'

'You have been hearing about the Nun of Kent.'

'How can I forget her? She insists on telling me about all her ecstasies and conversation with the dead – Wolsey, Warham, my father and, of course, the Virgin Mary – and how displeased the heavenly elite is with my marriage to Anne. She predicted all sorts of unpleasant consequences like losing my crown. What has she to do with my exchequer?'

'The Observant Friars are making use of her to cause discontent about your supremacy. They are a preaching order and it is almost impossible to prevent them from sounding off about your marriage to Anne and the break with Rome. You are aware, Sire, that there are almost 100,000 monks and friars in the kingdom who owe direct allegiance to the Pope and act as spies and supporters of your enemies. As Principal Secretary I must warn you that your supremacy of the Church of England will never become permanent nor reside in the hearts of your subjects unless you muzzle the regular clergy, especially the friars.'

'Over a year ago I said that I was determined that the vast wealth that has over the centuries been bestowed by Englishmen upon the Church should be carefully reviewed and inspected by the Crown. But nothing has happened. I need a new and vigorous man in charge. You, Thomas.'

'Then, Sire, if you approve, I would focus my efforts not on the Church as a whole but on the regular clergy – the friars and monks – whose wealth alone would resolve most of Your Majesty's financial difficulties. Their annual income is said to be greater than £170,000. That is more than all your own sources of funding added together. The money is important but more pressing is the war you are in effect waging with the regular clergy over their opposition to your supremacy and their loyalty to the Pope. They are spies, informers and secret enemies of the crown. They are "factious persons". They live by their own rules, are exempt from episcopal discipline and are papal spies. They have bowed to the royal supremacy and parliamentary legislation but they have not accepted the law of the land in their hearts. I quote one friar: he acknowledges "the king as Supreme Head of the Church for fear but cannot find in his conscience to believe it." I would advocate the dissolution and confiscation of all monastic lands, with their wealth and administration turned over to the Crown. But I emphasise a proviso: the monastic destruction must be done piecemeal, chapter house by chapter house. No one must be allowed to think that you have launched a war to destroy monasticism in England. We might well lose the battle if they did. At all costs the fight to maintain your supremacy and incidentally the financial profits from confiscated monastic lands must appear to the people to be isolated events and kept out of feudal and secular hands. Let the monks and friars fight their own battles but do not let their complaints turn into a general civil war. You might well lose such a civil war, but there is every chance you can win a monkish war. Start with the Friars Observant, that is where the Nun of Kent comes into the picture.'

'I agree the Observant Friars are a nest of traitors. Mercifully there are not many of them, only six chapters in England, but all are strategically placed – one is connected to my palace at Greenwich, another to my palace at Richmond. They are very close to the dowager princess and her daughter Mary, and for years have been the chaplains and advisers of royalty. Now I discover that they are secret creatures of Rome and traitors to their country.'

'You are already aware, Sire, of the truth about Elizabeth Barton, the so-called Holy Maid of Kent, who at eighteen fell ill and suffered trances and visions which rapidly turned treasonous as she reported that the heavenly city was adamantly opposed to both your title as Head of the Church and your new wife as Queen of England. Archbishop Warham sent five monks, two of whom were Observants, to investigate her creditability and pronounced her holy and "a person much in favour of God". The disease spread to Bishop John Fisher of Rochester who, as you well know, is a passionate friend of the dowager princess and the Pope, and even Sir Thomas More has been implicated. I started legal proceedings against them all, forced a public confession from the maid and some of her supporters that her visions and prophecies were all lies and fabrications. They were all executed last May. In the meantime the Observant Chapter at Greenwich began to openly preach against your supremacy and marriage, and fathers Peto and Forrest had to be imprisoned. The whole chapter seems to be thirsting for martyrdom.'

'Then give it to them and any other seditious monk,' was the king's brief reply.

Henry sat with an angry flush on his face that grew redder by the minute; Anne strode noisily about the room deliberately knocking into furniture and rattling the candlesticks and bric-a-brac. 'Henry,' she exclaimed, 'You know full well that there are four people in the kingdom who have refused the oath of succession and your supremacy of the Church who must be punished; your daughter Mary, the Dowager Princess of Wales, Bishop John Fisher, and Sir Thomas More.'

'Anne, for God's sake be reasonable. I can't execute Katherine, let alone my own daughter. All I can do is make their lives unpleasant and hope they will eventually come to their senses and obey me. Bishop Fisher may well lose his head. He has committed treason a dozen times over and has urged Emperor Charles to invade the country and relieve me of my crown. If the Pope goes through with his excommunication, Fisher's life will be forfeited. More is the stickiest traitor of the lot. His refusal to attend your coronation was a brazen defiance of my authority and a flagrant insult to you and I have neither forgiven nor forgotten. He languishes now in the Tower, where he will remain until he obliges his king and takes the oath. The trouble is by wrapping himself in the cloak of silence and refusing to explain why he will not take the oath he has committed misprision but not high treason. What is so baffling is that silence by law assumes affirmation. More is in fact saying he approves the oath but for personal reasons won't take it. We have had this conversation a dozen times before, so let us quit and allow me to go hunting.'

'I won't allow it! The law must be applied equally to all subjects including daughters and ex-wives of kings. I bet, should I ever inadvertently commit treason, you would not hesitate to take my head. Everybody knows that More's silence conceals treason and I want his head on a platter.'

'Anne, you are more vicious than Salome. You may well get your wish but don't blame me for the consequences. I am off to put on hunting gear,' and he exited banging the door.

Cromwell was sitting in his study at an ornate desk with a mother-of-pearl lift-up top and massive legs that he had taken great pains to purchase when the government sold off Cardinal Wolsey's property at York Place. With the possible exception of the magnificent opal ring he wore on his finger, which George Cavendish had sent him after the cardinal's death with the instructions that Wolsey had wanted Cromwell to wear it, he prized the desk above all his possessions. Together, desk and ring symbolised Cromwell's new status in life. The desk had been Wolsey's centre for ruling both State and Church; now it was once again the hub of governmental power. Although the king's confidential adviser was no longer Lord Chancellor, that position was held by his friend and minion Thomas Audley; Cromwell had been promoted to the office of the king's Principal Secretary, a position he coveted above all others for it was unhampered by history and tradition. He could make of it as he willed and override whomever he desired, even the Lord Chancellor, for Cromwell alone managed the king's calendar. Also, he had recently been appointed Vicar General for all ecclesiastical and spiritual affairs, a new office that went far beyond Wolsey's authority as cardinal legate. The ring was an ever-present reminder of the golden flow of wealth that had begun to pour into Cromwell's velvet pockets. Everyone who wanted something done or not done gave lavishly – from a side of beef, a dozen gull's eggs, an acre of prime land, or

£100 – to the man who controlled, and in some cases, made, the king's policies.

He was reading a letter from Thomas Bedyll, one of his most senior and trusted agents inspecting monasteries for corruption, malfeasance and superstition. He had just finished interviewing the Carthusian monks at the Charterhouse in London and demanding that they take the oath of succession and avow the king as Supreme Head of the Church of England. By August of 1534 Bedyll was having trouble with the Carthusians, especially with John Houghton the prior and Humphrey Middlemore the convent procurator, and reported:

I am right sorry to see the foolishness and obstinacy of diverse religious men so addicted to the Bishop of Rome and his usurped power, that they contemn all counsel and likewise jeopardy their bodies and souls and the suppression of their houses as careless men and willing to die. If it were not for the opinion which men had, and some yet have, in their apparent holiness, which is and was, for the most part, covert hypocrisy, it made no great matter what became of them so that their souls were saved. And as for my part, I would that all such obstinate persons of them, who be willing to die for the advancement of the Bishop of Rome's authority, were dead indeed by God's hand; no man should run wrongfully into calumny for their punishment. For the avoiding thereof I have taken some pains to reduce them from their errors, and will take more if I be commanded.

After a year of stalling, lukewarm acceptance of the king's marriage and open criticism of Henry as 'a king with a pope in his belly', John Houghton, Humphrey Middleton and two others openly defied the king's law and the royal supremacy, crying out, 'Let us die together in our integrity, and heaven and earth shall witness for us how unjustly we are cut off.'

Cromwell was now confronted with what to do with martyrs. He tried prolonged torture, monks chained by the neck to the wall, standing without food or drink to either die or apostate. Then in May of 1535 came formal and public execution in as horrible a way as the government could devise. Houghton and his three colleagues were chained to a sled still dressed in their monastic habits and dragged to Tyburn to be hung by the neck, cut down while still living, tied down spread-eagled, castrated, their genitals burned before their eyes, and disembowelled, and finally their bodies cut up for future display through the kingdom. The entire court was ordered to view the punishment so that no one forgot the dreadful consequence of treason. One of Prior Houghton's arms was pinioned to the entrance gate of his charterhouse priory in London; a gruesome message to those who were tempted to defy the royal supremacy.

As the official in charge, Cromwell had to watch the death agonies of the men he had commanded to be killed. He knew that there was no winning in this battle with martyrs willing to die. He also knew that no matter how silently or noisily they endured their fate, their deaths would correspond little to the way history would record the event. Hanging a victim by the neck even for a short time left him half strangled with swollen throat muscles making speech impossible, possibly even rendering him unable to scream when disembowelled. They were all in a state of extreme shock, unable to enact their assigned heroic script. Yet authoritative descriptions would without fail maintain that the martyrs died with a smile on their faces, murmuring as the knife ripped their bodies, 'My, but that smarts'. It was all a performance scripted for the benefit of the living, an event over which Cromwell had no control. He swore to himself that he would keep martyrdom to a minimum but he had little say over what the king might command.

Cromwell gave orders to his retainers to meet him at the entrance of Austin Friars, a three-storey mansion on more than two acres of prime land once owned by the Augustinian Friars. Lavishly rebuilt, it was the largest and priciest private home in London, replete with tennis court, bowling alley and walking gardens. In an age when political power required the visual and costly attire of pomp and circumstance Cromwell needed a magnificent London residence to display and prove his authority. The Principal Secretary was now headed for the Tower of London to meet up with Thomas Howard, Duke of Norfolk, the most powerful nobleman in the land, who, as Cromwell mounted his horse, was being rowed down the river from Hampton Court, to resolve the thorniest problem still remaining from the King's Great Matter – what to do with Sir Thomas More.

The two men met at Traitor's Gate and walked to More's cell in the fortress. Norfolk was tall, angular and strangely without substance, his sad eyes looking out upon a world he failed to understand or like. He was the product of history and little else, certainly not of education, talent or ingenuity. His grandfather, the first Duke of Norfolk, had died at Bosworth Field trying to prevent the Tudor line from establishing its dynasty on the throne. His father as a consequence had survived three years' imprisonment in the Tower where the duke now stood, and learned a lesson he passed on to his son: the Tudors were here to stay and had God on their side; they were kings by divine and military right. What had not been explained to the son was that power no longer rested with the aristocracy ruling by right of the sword and divine decree, but by the likes of Cardinal Wolsey, the son of a butcher, and more recently by Thomas Cromwell, the offspring of a brewer and blacksmith, both men who appreciated that knowledge, paperwork and Machiavellian calculation were the secrets of political success. The ducal title had been re-established when Norfolk's father had proved his loyalty to the Tudor throne by resoundingly defeating a Scottish army and its king at the Battle of Flodden in 1513; Thomas Howard was now the second Tudor Duke of Norfolk.

As the duke and Principal Secretary entered More's cell furnished with a cot, work table covered with writing materials, two chairs and several piles of books, the prisoner stepped forward and politely said, 'Good Morrow, Your Grace and Master Secretary,' then promptly sat back down again at the table. 'You come to reform me or harangue me?' The speaker had been a handsome man but sickness and imprisonment had turned him into a haggard old man of fifty-seven years. Nevertheless the eyes and mouth retained their merry twinkle and firm line. Sir Thomas always looked at you as if he were probing your soul and judging the calibre of your spiritual worth. An aura of brooding yet mocking intelligence emanated from a lined and scarred face that made the viewer feel deeply inadequate.

'I read your *Utopia*,' proclaimed Norfolk as if he were a maître d' announcing the arrival of royalty.

Since the book was written back in 1515, almost twenty years before, More did not know how to respond, but being a master of decorum, possessing the ability to adapt to time, place and persons, he simply said: 'I hope you enjoyed it.'

'I especially liked the part about divorce. You say Utopians can get a divorce for either adultery or incompatibility. No nonsense about the sanctity and permanence of marriage. I would have ended my marriage long ago on both counts if I could have persuaded my wife to agree.'

Thomas Cromwell broke into whatever discourse Norfolk had planned to deliver on the blessings of divorce. 'His Grace has inadvertently raised an important subject, Sir Thomas: consistency, or more accurately, your lack of it. You refuse to voice your approval of the king's annulment of his marriage yet you offer divorce to your Utopians. You refuse to take the oath of succession on the grounds that it requires you to approve all the enactments and legislation that Parliament has passed during the past five years. You say that you will obey all laws duly signed by the king and legislated by Lords and Commons but as a government official and one-time Lord Chancellor you are now refusing to obey your king's order to take a corporal oath proving you a loyal subject. As you put it, "a subject is no longer bounden to the keeping of the law; now he must swear that every law is well made". The law is explicit: those who argue that they are "not bound to declare their thought and conscience" have committed high treason. Yet you state that Utopians who even think, not enact, but think adultery, warrant punishment on the argument that the thought must be father to the act. Is taking an oath to the succession of the throne anything more or less than your own condemnation of adulterous thinking? Is it too much to expect the dutiful subject to love, to obey and honour our prince not only outwardly in our bodies but also inwardly in our hearts without dissimulation or feigning? More extraordinarily, you grant freedom of religion to your make-believe world, allowing sun, moon, planet worshippers and a pandemic force called the Father of All, but as Lord Chancellor you turned the cellars of your house at Chelsea into a torture chamber for those you labelled heretics.'

'You prove my inconsistency from words of fantasy written twenty years ago! Surely, Thomas, you can do better than that. You fail to acknowledge that words are the product of changing times, place and circumstance. Martin Luther had not posted his ninety-five theses in 1515 and advertised his pernicious heresies to all of Europe. Today Luther has let Satan loose upon the Christian world and evil flourishes as it has never blossomed before. The Lutheran heresy maintains that the true Church exists neither in a sacerdotal priesthood, nor in sacramental ancient customs and cathedrals cut in stone, but solely in the hearts of the believers, inspired by a deity who blesses and enlightens a small number of the elect and leaves the rest in satanic darkness. Such a view makes a mockery of 1,500 years of history, turns Christ into a liar, and breeds civil wars and spiritual anarchy. No compromise is possible when Satan is on the rampage as he has been for the past ten years, and I am proud that my poor home has been a place where heretics have been persuaded to renounce their evil ways. You say, that I have "fed the stake with heretics". I say that I have saved immortal souls from hell. A faith that lacks the proof of centuries and the sacred ritual of time-honoured custom, and must rely on the word of a filthy German monk and his concubine wife, who calls herself a nun, is a leaderless morass open to the uncertainty of every wind of doctrine, and will reduce everything to doubt. Mine is the fate of Cassandra: she possessed the power of prophecy, but nobody believed her. Satan is a crafty beast. I allow my Utopian priests to marry because it is as honourable a state in God's eyes as chastity but see what the devil does with the permission: Martin Luther marries a nun under the name of wedlock in open incestuous lechery without care or shame. Now that is disgusting and vile. Give the devil an inch and he will inevitably take an ell. You cannot compromise with Satan.'

'Well spoken, Sir Thomas, and you might well have added that your Utopians would never have countenanced the king's marriage to Mistress Boleyn, his acceptance of the title of Supreme Head of the Church of England, and his refusal to abide by the authority of the Bishop of Rome. All the actions of the Reformation Parliament would have been void because all Utopians think alike and therefore act alike. They have abolished freedom of thought and action in order to achieve intellectual and spiritual security that stems from absolute consensus. As you put it in your treatise, "A kingdom in all its parts is like a man; it is held together by natural affection, bonds as light as air but strong as iron." As in the body politic every cell is conditioned to do its duty because God has created it to think only in terms of the greater good of the whole body. Is this so different from the king's policy of achieving a kingdom filled with loving and dutiful subjects who have learned a "new found article of faith, that a statute made by the authority of the entire realm cannot err". To put it slightly differently, it is no longer sufficient to simply obey the law, it is demanded that everyone, including you, should approve it and engrave it upon your hearts in an oath of loyalty.'

'Clearly I should not debate with yet another lawyer, of which there are far too many in the world.'

'Tell me, Master More, exactly why you think you are incarcerated here in this ill-furnished space fifteen by fifteen foot square and very likely risking your life either by continued lack of sunshine or possibly by the executioner's blade? What holds you here: your soul or your conscience? Are the two distinguishable from one another? Or is it possibly your sense that your God, your faith, and your Church are endangered? In truth, are we not, Sir Thomas, really speaking about your pride, your ego?'

'Here, I have forced one of you to stand by remaining seated.' He rose and offered his seat to the duke. Cromwell guessed his hidden purpose was to gain time to consider his answer to the secretary's question. He had not liked Cromwell's suggestion that pride was at the heart of his defiance of his prince. 'In good faith, Cromwell, I see no good reason for my harsh treatment. I do nobody harm, I say none harm, I think none harm but wish everybody good. If this be not enough to keep a man alive, I long not to live.'

'Then I will have to tell you. You think that in wrapping yourself in silence you have found a way of baulking the government's determination to prove your disloyalty. But you are wrong, Master More, the crown has two indisputable acts on your part to prove the maliciousness of your thoughts. First, you were requested to appear at Queen Anne's coronation with every other loyal subject of the kingdom. You were even provided with money for a new gown that you accepted but you stayed at home, a dog in the manger unwilling to celebrate your queen's coronation. That was sheer pettiness on your part, displaying publically that you do not regard Anne to be the legal wife of the king and therefore not a queen. You are right, it did no one any good but it did you great harm. You won the contempt and hatred of the queen who has been spending the past year persuading the king that you should be executed in full, hideous high treason style. Then there is your refusal to take the oath of succession attached to the Act of Succession which requires all loyal subjects "down to the village constable and priest" to make a corporal oath that they shall "truly, firmly and constantly without fraud or guile observe to their uttermost powers the whole effect and content of the Act of Succession granting parliamentary sanction to the queen's marriage and naming the baby Elizabeth legal heir, and all other acts and statutes made since the beginning of this present parliament." I think I have the wording right, I wrote it myself.'

'You are absolutely right, Cromwell, not going to Anne's coronation was a petty act and a serious mistake but I enjoyed every minute of it. As for the oath, you know full well that my body belongs solely to the king and would never act or speak against him. Except for my soul, I would willingly give up everything to avoid a single "displeasant look" from His Highness. You are asking me to risk my soul's perpetual damnation by forcing me to take of the oath of succession.'

'It is exactly that exception, your soul or conscience or whatever you call it, that is causing the difficulty. To whom does your soul belong? To the king and the kingdom that protected you and gave you a name; to the Pope and the enemies of the realm, or to yourself, a single Christian who can say with as much conviction as the king himself: "Though the law of every man's conscience be but a private court, yet it is the highest and supreme court for judgment and justice?"'

'Conscience, Master Secretary, is the possession of every man's own self, his persona, and I condemn the conscience of no man who swears to the oath of succession. I have never withdrawn any man from taking the corporal oath, nor ever advised any to refuse it, but left every man to his own conscience. And me thinketh in good faith every man should leave me to mine. I will even explain the troubles I have with the oath in writing if the council will grant me full immunity from the law, for my reasons might be construed as treason.'

'That, the council should not and will not grant. Rule out any grant of immunity, Sir Thomas.'

'Then, if I cannot speak or explain without endangering my life, no one has a right to call my refusal to take the oath stubbornness or obstinacy, and it is certainly not treason. It is simply the most sensible way of saving my life.'

Norfolk could not keep quiet in the face of such disloyal and mulish wilfulness: 'Surely a private conscience of a single man cannot stand against the truth embedded in the great council of the realm and the conscience of a divine right king?'

'But, Your Grace, I do not stand alone. I have the "general council of all Christendom" and the consensus of 1,500 years of history on my side which overwhelms the silly opinions of a single kingdom.'

'You may claim whatever you want,' Cromwell thoughtfully said, 'but you are treading dangerously close to what Clement of Alexandria warned in the third century: "Whosoever does not avoid persecution but out of daring presents himself for capture becomes an accomplice in the crime of the persecutors." You are risking suicide, Sir Thomas, to safeguard your soul. Wasn't it John of Salisbury who said "Truly all enthusiasm, especially martyrdom, is the foe of salvation and all excess is a fault; nothing is worse than the immoderate practice of good works"?'

Sir Thomas had turned a lighter pale than the prison white that was his normal Tower colouring. 'I have not been a man of such holy living as might be bold enough to offer myself to death, lest God for my presumption might suffer me to fall and therefore I put myself forward, but draw back. Howbeit if God draws me to it Himself, then trust I in his great mercy that He shall not fail to give me grace and strength. The citadel of self, one's own private conscience, cannot be ignored. No matter how deeply a person tries to wrap himself and his conscience in the consensus of all Christendom and shield it with the voice of 1,500 years of history, the I, the self, is clearly manifest. As St Paul said, 'Every man stands or falls before his own Lord, alone and by himself.' Cromwell sighed to himself; More was being just as individualistic in his convictions as any Utopian punished for individual possessiveness in refusing to exchange his house with his neighbour at command of the State.

'I should warn you, Sir Thomas, the Crown's patience is at an end, and Richard Riche, whom you know, will shortly be here to remove your remaining books, pen and paper. Henceforth you will only have your conscience, yourself, to talk or write to.'

Within the hour of the duke and Cromwell's departure, Sir Richard arrived to remove everything from More's cell except the furniture and a few pieces of clothing. While his men were stripping the table of its writing equipment and books, Sir Richard, being a cheerful man with no strong political or religious convictions but spilling over with optimism, suggested that More reconsider his position, cease his obstinacy and take the oath of loyalty. More replied in his usual polite if obscure manner: 'Your conscience shall save you and my conscience shall save me.' Then Riche, assuring the prisoner that their conversation was private and phrased in the hypothetical language of legal debate, continued his conversation by asking, 'Admit there were, sir, an Act of Parliament that all the realm should take me for king. Would not you, Master More, take me for king?' Sir Thomas assured him that he thought the proposition improbable but 'Yes, he would accept him as king,' but he countered in this game of propositions, 'Suppose the Parliament should make a law that God should not be God, would you then, Mr Riche, say God were not God?' Sir Richard immediately complained that such a statement changed the terms of the debate. 'Not only can't you legislate a negative, but also Parliament could not abolish a power over which it had no control.' He then offered what he called a halfway measure: 'What if Parliament created the king Supreme Head of the Church? Why should you not, Master More, affirm and accept him to be so in exactly the same way you accepted me as king?' To the question More replied 'The cases are not alike; the subject cannot be obligated to give his consent to such a thing in Parliament. Though the king may be so accepted in England, most foreign lands do not accept the same.' The date was June the twelfth and Cromwell heard about the conversation within minutes of the spoken word. He instantly recognised More's fatal error. The answer More gave was without reference to any hypothetical limitations and demonstrated a foreign preference. The words as reported by Sir Richard Riche were high treason, and the ex-Lord Chancellor was brought to trial within twenty days. It only took the jury fifteen minutes to find him guilty.

More's answer to the verdict was to remind the jury and his judges that St Paul before his conversion to Christianity had been instrumental in the death of the martyr Saint Stephen, and that now 'the two men were holy saints in heaven and friends for ever, and so I shall therefore right heartily pray, that though your lordships have now on earth been judges to my condemnation, we may yet hereafter in heaven all merrily meet together to our lasting salvation.' It was a javelin thrust directed at the judge and jury sending them to hell unless they, like St Paul, joined More in death and martyrdom. After the execution that Cromwell dutifully attended, he sadly shook his head in the rain that had been pouring down all day, and said to nobody in particular, 'What a dreadful waste of magnificent intelligence. Everything he did, he did superbly well, his martyrdom was near perfection.'

Cromwell had made arrangements with Mark Smeaton to meet him at the White Horse Tavern down the street from where Thomas lived. Mark had moved into the queen's new residence at Whitehall that was in walking distance of the tavern. They sat at a secluded table, great beakers of mead in hand waiting the prospect of a satisfying meal. Thomas broke the friendly silence. 'What do you think of monks and friars?'

Mark smiled and said, 'What do you want, the quantitative or qualitative answer?'

'It doesn't matter.'

'Well, the quantitative reply is "Not at all. They do not in any way impinge upon my life." The qualitative answer is "Not much, they are mostly hypocrites claiming a higher, better, and more godly life but are actually wallowing in a very worldly existence."'

'We are on the same track, except that I think about monks and friars all the time – you know that the king has appointed me Vicar General of all ecclesiastical and spiritual affairs and the Act of Supremacy places all monastic foundation directly under the protection and administration of the Crown, not the authority of the secular clergy and Archbishop of Canterbury.'

'What is your problem then? You can do with the worthless old oaks what you will – dissolve them or reform them.'

Cromwell sighed. 'I do not worry about the fate of the monasteries but the fate of my reputation. I am becoming the ogre and villain of the piece. My agents are canvassing the land, revealing the superstitions that monks have perpetrated on the kingdom, the multiple abuses they have practised and the wealth they have squandered on silk bedding, daily feasting on meat without regard to holy days, and the satisfaction of carnal desires with nuns and monks or worse with one another. I am forever being told that the spirit of martyrdom is dead in the midst of modern worldliness and secularism but neither the Observant Friars nor the Carthusian monks have shown any reluctance in choosing the path of martyrdom and enduring the pain. I am not sure the king's side in this struggle of rival consciences and beliefs can endure many more martyrs. The greater their pain, the more triumphant their victory. When death in every horrible form becomes proof of the truth of their faith, martyrs become a powerful weapon, and I get blamed for all their agonies as well as all the failing and abuses that my agents have perpetrated in conducting this war on monasticism.'

'You are now, my friend, actually admitting that you and the king are conducting a military campaign to destroy the regular clergy both legally and financially.'

'It is getting increasingly difficult to conceal that truth.'

'Then go whole hog and stop blaming yourself for all the pain and sorrow that warfare entails. You are now the top general, the chief of staff. And generals don't go about assuming responsibility for every horror or misconduct done by common soldiers. During the Hundred Years' War, English soldiers committed endless atrocities, but no one holds Henry V responsible. He got credit for the successes of war, not its fury or sorrow. The same applies to you. Close your mind to cruelty of war and concentrate on the money you are endowing the royal exchequer with, the pleasure you are giving the king, and the divine truth that what you are doing is part and parcel of God's design.'

'I hope, Mark, you are right; it certainly makes me feel better, but this war on monkery is a religious conflict, not a secular or feudal or chivalric war. So far most of the historians have been in league with the monks and friars, and I don't expect to receive fair treatment in their reports on what they pass on as history. Moreover, the fate of the monasteries has placed me at odds with the queen. From the start she has taken a holier than thou attitude, monks and friars must be replaced with expensive college dons and even more expensive new dioceses with gorgeous cathedrals. Both I and the king thought the Crown had been sufficiently generous to education in allowing Wolsey's Cardinal College to continue existence as King's College.' We are both of the opinion that the vast wealth of the monasteries should go to the royal exchequer to endow the king's supremacy. John Skip, the queen's almoner and favourite chaplain, threw down the gauntlet in a long and angry sermon accusing the king's council of plundering the Church of its wealth and property. He never would have spoken as he did without the queen's consent. He defended every ancient and senseless Church ritual as if it was the Holy Grail and not outmoded and senseless claptrap.'

'The woman sounds like a first-class pest. What are you going to do about her?' Before Cromwell could answer their food arrived, and he limited himself to merely saying, 'The grub here is as near to perfection as is humanly possible to achieve. No one is trying to mould it into some preconceived truth.'

CHAPTER V

The Self-Fashioned Man

Of the seven men invited to dinner Mark Smeaton was the first to arrive. He did so in a whirlwind of colours astride a handsome Spanish steed that danced, not walked, its rider through the gates to Austin Friars. He was accompanied by a matching horse and rider dressed in freshly cut livery to accompany him home after dark. If apparel and a well-liveried servant were any evidence, Mark Smeaton was knocking loudly on the door of gentility.

The guests were seated around the dining-room table at Austin Friars. They sat on chairs with comfortable padded seats made of horsehair covered with elaborate needle-point, a sure sign of Thomas Cromwell's rising status in society; no stools or benches for the man who held the king's highest and most powerful offices – not only Principal Secretary and Vicar General for ecclesiastical and spiritual affairs, but now also Master of the Rolls, a useful office if one ever needed to tamper with history. The occasion was Hans Holbein's request for help in completing the portraits of Jean de Dinteville, the young French ambassador to the English court, and his friend and visitor George de Selve, Bishop of Lavaur. Holbein wanted advice on what symbols and devices to include in the picture to make the portraits more true to the world and times in which the two men lived. Cromwell orchestrated the party of close friends and admirers of Holbein who would enjoy talking art and philosophy with the painter.

Cromwell started proceedings by introducing his guests. 'Seated in the middle is my old friend Hans Holbein, whom I first knew in 1526 when we both worked for the great cardinal. He is the Apelles of our times; his realism, symbolism and ability to bring mankind to life in two-dimensional form are spectacular. Sitting next to him on his right is another, even older, friend, Mark Smeaton, who started his career as I did with the cardinal, and as you all know is now one of the queen's prize singers and musicians. What you do not know is he is a talented amateur painter himself and has much in common with Hans. Next to Mark is George Cavendish, usher to Wolsey and now a quiet country gentleman who finds every excuse to come to town. I believe his son, aged twenty, is in trouble and needs powerful friends; thus George has come to me. I promised George that he need not worry about his offspring's troubles. To Holbein's left sits Sir Richard Riche, Solicitor General and excellent lawyer, an old and useful friend who is a client of everyone with a modicum of power. I predict he will survive us all. Beside Riche is my adopted son and blood nephew, Richard Cromwell, who is my highly efficient secretary as well as a passionate horseman and happy only when he is in the tilting yard. His aim in life is to unseat the king; from his horse that is, not his throne. The empty seat beside me is reserved for Sir Thomas Wyatt, who is always late to every junction except possibly his lover's bed.

'Before getting to the real purpose of this dinner – Holbein's portrait of two Frenchmen – I suggest we start by sampling my chef's food. He is French and a master of the culinary arts. I believe he has ordered up as a first course a fat and succulent goose replete with a multitude of French sauces – the best of English-French dining.' The goose was consumed with gusto and full-mouth babblings of appreciation. As the second and fish course of salmon trout appeared so did Sir Thomas Wyatt, with loud apologies for being late and how annoyed he was with the Queen Anne.

'Sit down, Thomas, next to me in this chair kept only for you, and tell us about our controversial queen.'

'She entered her receiving room this morning in an appallingly bad temper, fresh from an encounter with the Lady Mary. She was itching to quarrel with everybody including her husband. The Lady Mary, violently against her will, had been assigned as an attendant to the Princess Elizabeth's nursery. The drama started when Anne, who was visiting her daughter, was told that the young girl had dutifully curtsied to her without her realising it. Anne had immediately sent her stepdaughter an apology for not having noticed such a promising sign of respect for her position as queen and offered immediate friendship to the young girl. Mary's reply was unspeakably rude: she assured the "Lady Anne Boleyn," notice the phraseology, that she "acknowledged no other queen but her mother, nor esteemed them my friends who are not hers." And her curtsey, she claimed, was to God, her best friend and creator, not Anne.'

'It sounds to me as if Her Highness had cause to be outraged,' said Cromwell. 'That girl is even more stubborn and bigoted than her mother.'

'True,' laughed Wyatt, 'but the queen didn't have to take her displeasure and anger out on everybody in the room. She announced that the Lady Mary was "my death, and I am hers". What she meant by that no one dares to think.'

'I agree,' Cromwell broke in, 'Chapuys, the Imperial ambassador, lives next door; the walls of my dining room have ears, and little is said that the ambassador does not hear. Servants will talk to one another. So let's drop the subject of what the queen really meant. There are ferocious laws that punish people for disparaging the queen or speaking ill of her.'

Wyatt had no intention of allowing his host to curtail his rich court gossip that was too good to be smothered by political caution. 'Before we do, let me tell you what else she said about becoming the country's regent should Henry visit the King of France in Calais. She said that if given regental powers she would immediately have both Katherine and Mary executed for refusing to take the oath of succession, and if she failed in doing this she would have them starved to death. When her brother, Lord Rochford, interrupted and told his sister that her words were silly and dangerous and to cease her angry ranting, Anne answered that she "did not care what Henry thought," even if she were "burnt alive for her actions". Anne is obsessed with the legend that a mythical English queen was once burned at the stake, I think for witchcraft. She is forever talking about the poor lady.'

'That is no way for a queen to talk. If she does not mend her lips,' said Richard Cromwell, 'she is less likely to burn than to die on the scaffold minus her head.'

'You make a good point, son,' Cromwell said. 'The world is filled with people who have no sense of decorum, their words never fit the occasion. The queen is one of the worst examples and she lacks the excuse of never having been trained in decorum and rhetoric; she uses words and metaphors to shock and amuse without regard for how people will later understand her speech and which are often hopelessly inappropriate to what she is trying to say. I agree, it may someday get her into serious political trouble.'

Wyatt continued with his story. 'At this point the king entered the chamber en route to the hunt. Immediately, Anne picked a quarrel with him and began scolding

Henry for secretly favouring his daughter Mary over her daughter Elizabeth, and failing to punish his ex-wife for her treasonous refusal to accept Anne as queen and the baby Elizabeth as rightful heir to the throne. Both subjects were voiced *ad nauseam* by the queen. Usually Henry is longsuffering and ignores his wife's nagging but today he was in an equally vile mood and turned on Anne with a blast of frightening words: he told Anne, "You must shut your eyes and endure, just like others who were worthier than you, and you ought to know that I could humiliate you in only a moment longer than it had taken to exalt you." Then he added that she had good reason to be content with what he had done for her, which he would not do again, if he were starting afresh. She should remember where she had come from. Both king and queen left the room banging the door, one to hunt, the other to sulk. Not a pretty picture.'

Cromwell again injected the need for a change of topic. 'I see the roast coming so let us cease the court chatter. While eating beef in the French style let me ask Sir Thomas Wyatt a question about his poetry. Tom, I know your verses well even though they have never been published in print, and I can recite the names of at least six of your poems bemoaning your love life.' Cromwell rattled the titles off from memory: '"An Earnest Suit to his Unkind Mistress not to Forsake Him," "The Lady to Answer Directly with Yea or Nay," "The Lover Complaineth the Unkindness of his Love," "The Lover Describeth his Being Stricken with Sight of his Love," "The Lover Forsaketh his Unkind Love," and the best of them all, "They Flee from Me." Now, Wyatt, here is my question: are these poems about a single passionate love affair worthy of six verses dealing with your rejection by a lady we all recognise, or are they about six different beauties who failed to respond to your advances. If the latter, all rejections by different ladies, what happens to your reputation as God's gift to womankind and your fame as a modern Eros, the son of Aphrodite, charming and bedding every woman he encounters? Six failures, given your renown that you will go to the end of the earth and face any challenge for the sake of the female gender, is not a good average, and I find it hard to believe.'

Wyatt combined a grin with a scowl and said, 'Cromwell, you are baiting me. I am between the devil and the deep blue sea. It might cost me my head if I dared admit to a love dedicated to a single mistress, and as you suggest my fame is hopelessly diminished if I admit to six rejections. I don't think, Thomas, you really expect me to answer but I will rehearse you a verse that you have never heard; it was composed only this afternoon. It is a poetic translation of Petrarch's "Una candida cerva". It is about hunting a hind.

'Whoso list to hunt, I know where is an hind,
But as for me, alas, I may no more:
The vain travail hath wearied me sore.
I am of them that farthest cometh behind.
Yet may I by no means my wearied mind

> Draw from the Deer: but as she fleeth afore,
> Fainting I follow. I leave off therefore,
> Since in a net I seek to hold the wind.
> Who list her hunt I put him out of doubt,
> As well as I may spend his time in vain:
> And, graven with Diamonds, in letters plain
> There is written her fair neck round about:
> *Noli me tangere* [touch me not] for Caesar's I am,
> And wild for to hold though I seem tame.'

Wyatt had scarcely finished his recital when Richard Cromwell spoke up. 'I don't get it. What has a wild hind got to do with the queen?'

'It's a metaphor, Richard,' answered his father. 'If you are not flattering a lady or when speaking of politically dangerous topics, it is always safest to conceal your message behind a faux literary device such as a metaphor. Speaking solely for myself, Wyatt, I think you are well out from under the Boleyn magic though your verse seems to indicate the break is only partial. It is far better to leave the taming of the wild hind to the king, although judging from your description of their recent quarrel, he is having his troubles. The lady is indeed wild, the woman is forever falling away from tameness and civilised discourse. Her violence is close to madness and is a danger to all codes of sexual conduct, social intercourse and stable government. Let the king handle her.'

'Don't worry,' laughed Wyatt, 'Henry will be back in her arms tomorrow morning happy as a baby milking his mother's breasts. She still possesses marvellous sex appeal.'

'Very possibly,' growled Cromwell, 'but remember that the baby grows into the determined and ruthless man. But once again enough of the Boleyn saga. We have finished the beef and have had dessert. It is time for Hans Holbein and his picture. Hans, tell us about its provenance.'

Holbein rose from the table and drew from the corner of the room an easel with the double portraits proudly displayed. Darkness had encompassed the room and the table candle filled the space with a warm but unstable light that revealed the rigid shapes of Ambassador Jean de Dinteville and Bishop Georges de Selve leaning against a waist-high cabinet with an oriental carpet draped over the top, empty of all clutter except for an open book of Martin Luther's shortened version of the Ten Commandments and his translation of the hymn 'Veni Sancte Spiritus' on the only shelf. 'Jean de Dinteville,' Hans said, 'represents the French king at the English court and is a young, rising and wealthy young man from an important family. He commissioned the painting and insisted on the Lutheran manuscript, which says a lot about his religious preference. He gave me detailed instructions about the quality and flamboyance of his dress, and was adamant about the skull or 'death's-head' medallion on his cap. His personal motto is 'Remember thou must die.' He insisted that I display his order of St Michael. It is a bit of chivalric nonsense left over from the medieval past but still carries great honour and respect in aristocratic circles. Why George de Selve is in town for his portrait is something of a mystery. He is a friend of Jean's and possibly carried instructions from the French king. He too comes from an important and wealthy family but being an ecclesiastic his clothing is more subdued but equally expensive. All I know about him is that he was elevated to a bishop at the ridiculous age of eighteen. It is my understanding that you in this room have met Dinteville and may have valuable information about his interests so I can fill the cabinet and its shelf with symbols of his life.'

Mark Smeaton immediately spoke up. 'I met Dinteville several times in the queen's chambers. He regards himself as a talented lutenist and fancies himself on the flute as worthy of Pan. I thought him a better flute player than lutenist. Possibly a bundle of flutes and a lute with a broken string might represent the quality of his music.'

'You are being uncharitable towards the man, but I agree with you that he is hardly a modest Frenchman,' commented Cromwell. 'I can speak, however, to his interest in both astronomy and architecture. I have had lengthy diplomatic business with him and it was forever spilling over into philosophical discussions about astronomy and architecture.'

'He likes maps,' broke in Richard Riche, 'so load the cabinet with celestial and earthly globes, but be sure to predominately display England and Ireland. There is far too much Gallic trivia in the picture already.'

'I vote for a carpenter's compass and right angle,' added George Cavendish 'and for good measure a torquetum, which no one will recognise, and a universal equinoctial sun dial and a Shepard's dial.'

'What is a torquetum?' asked Cromwell's son.

'I believe it is a device to measure the course of planetary movement,' answered Cavendish. 'What about something to display his mastery of mathematics but not too difficult, possibly a commercial handbook. That should fill up your empty space nicely.'

'But not the space on the elegant mosaic floor in the foreground,' warned Mark. 'Mr Holbein, I have a suggestion that will reveal your extraordinary artistic talent and at the same time vastly enrich and deepen the meaning of your picture. Place an anamorphosis, in the shape of a giant skull, in front of the table on the floor to shock Dinteville and Selve out of their complacency and pride in having accomplished so much in their short lives. They appear far too pleased with themselves. An anamorphosis is the perfect device; the death's-head can't be seen by either the outside viewer or by the two smug young men in the portrait but it is in fact so close and so dominant that they will stumble over it if they move. And the outside viewer can only transform what looks like a vague and misty disk into a skull's head by turning the picture to the side and looking at it on the bias from the extreme left or right depending on which direction the skull is looking.'

'Brilliant,' said Cromwell. 'A trick of the eye will transform an interesting painting into a masterpiece.

The portrait will be changed from one of passing social interest into a shocking *tour de force* dealing not only with the terrifying brevity and frailty of life but also with the multiple achievements of mankind. The mind and imagination of man becomes the measure of all things. All else, Protestant versus Catholic, State versus Church, heaven and hell, God's justice as opposed to his mercy, all recede into the background. The self-defined man stands supreme. Sir Thomas More would have been shocked to his hair shirt at the triumph of possessive individualism. Wyatt, you are our expert on the self-fashioned individual. In a sense even in your penitential poems where man wallows in sin and seeks absolution and consolation by humbling himself before the divine dominance there is an undercurrent of human pride, the arrogant suggestion that God may need man more than man needs God. Man is both contrite and importunate. He makes a good case for himself before God, yet still accepts his ethical bankruptcy. You have him confess:

> 'Thy majesty so from my mind was gone:
> This know I and repent. Pardon thou then,
> For wilful malice led me not the way
> So much as hath the flesh drawn me apart.'

'No comment, Thomas. You have opened wide the doors of hell. No one wants to enter,' replied the versifier.

'If you have introduced death into the foreground to dominate human existence, don't you have to introduce God?' inquired young Richard Cromwell. 'I don't find him anywhere except in a tiny crucifix hanging on the background curtain that can only be seen with a magnifying lens. Doesn't He deserve greater attention?'

'God is where he belongs,' said his father, 'in the achievements of man, in the music, buildings, mathematical formulas and the advancing knowledge of mankind. Wasn't it Marsilio Ficino who wrote that since man has observed the order of the heavens, and with what measures they produce, who could then deny that man possesses as it were almost the same genius as the Author of the heavens? And who could deny that man could somehow also make the heavens, could he only obtain the instruments and heavenly material, since now he makes them, though of a different material, but still with a very similar purpose.'

George Cavendish broke the silence that followed Cromwell's calling upon the authority of Marsilio Ficino and the Italian priest's use of magic and astrology. 'I object,' shouted Wolsey's one-time usher. 'I object strenuously. You have reduced God to a human appendage, a product of man's mind. I am not a great scholar or world actor. You all have talents, as musicians, painters, scholars, wheelers and shakers of state. I have none of these. I represent the common man, and I ask you what has happened to my God, the God I worship? Where in the picture, and more important, in our discussion this evening is the Old Testament God of wrath and vengeance, where is the God who created green grass and twinkling stars, where is the God who made Adam, who placed temptation in Eve's path, who possessed the foreknowledge that Cain would murder Abel and bring violence into the world, and above all, where is the God who sent his only son into the world to save mankind from himself and who makes a mockery of your filthy death's-head?'

Strangely it was the usually quiet and non-controversial Richard Riche who answered. 'Mr Cavendish, you forget that God made man in his own image. As a consequence, we must be part god, part divine. Is it then unacceptable to say that God needs man both to worship Him and to bring about his ultimate purpose as much as man needs God to understand His universe and the meaning of existence?'

'Therefore,' added Wyatt, 'we have, in fact, diminished God, and that is something of a contradiction in terms: an omnipotent deity with absolute power and full foreknowledge of all things and complete authority to change events, and a restrained deity dependent on man to do most of the job by exercising his own creativity and imagination. We may have to choose between one and the other, and if it is a God dependent on his own creation then we have come close to advocating that new-fangled word coined recently by Sir John Cheke – atheism. Literally it means "without god" but used according to Cheke to describe people who do not "care whether there be a God or no, or whether God will recompense good men with good things and bad men with what is evil." Even the queen's chaplain, Hugh Latimer, has said that there are those in England who claim there is no human soul that is eternal, but like a dog, it dies with the body, going neither to heaven or hell.'

'To speak frankly,' said Cromwell, 'I too am a little worried by the concept of Heaven. I am perfectly willing to accept Hell as the proper place for a large portion of mankind and as the support and necessary negation of heaven, but paradise itself seems to me to be a very uncertain place. We are told that heaven houses our loved ones, but after twenty years will I continue to love them or will they love me? There are lots of my ancestors I do not want to meet again under any circumstances, including my father who was a horrid man. Will these loved ones look and act as they did on earth? In the case of my grandmother, would she continue to be old and senile? Hans, as a painter you should be able to answer this, how old do you make your painted inhabitants of heaven?'

'That's easy,' answered Hans, 'they are in a state of perfection, and that, we all know, is the age of Christ when he died. So they look thirty-three or four; all are exactly the same. Hell is far more of a challenge; there, individuality is rampant. Each agonising body is individually enduring his or her own unique punishment. Haven't you notice that all ancient tombstone effigies never look excessively young or old or sickly as they were in real life. They all appear vigorously middle aged. Hell is far more interesting to paint than heaven.'

'You know,' interrupted Cavendish, 'we are straying from the subject if there ever was one. We started with the simple task of helping Holbein here to fill his shelves; then we got distracted by the death-heads and the presence of death in the midst of life. Finally, we slipped into theology and God's role in the universe, then something called atheism, and now Heaven. I think that is far enough. I for one am off to bed. Master Holbein, you have achieved a remarkable masterpiece and I congratulate you.'

Three weeks later the Principal Secretary had business on the Strand and stopped in at Holbein's lodgings, close enough to the king's palace and Whitehall but distant enough to prevent nagging clients from insisting on daily progress reports. Cromwell had with him Sir Thomas Wyatt, who had insisted on viewing the new version of *The Ambassadors* and continuing their theological conversation with the painter. The anamorphic death's-head was finished and Holbein was enthusiastically grateful. 'That young man Mark Smeaton is a genius. His only defect is that he prefers listening to his own voice and strumming on the lute to studying the laws of perspective. He can actually paint an anamorphosis himself without my help. I don't know why I didn't think of the device myself. I am deep into my series on the Dance of Death and the folly of most human endeavours. I am still fascinated by our dining-room conversation but deeply disturbed by it. Do you really think we are all believers in atheism without our knowing it? We could be burned at the stake for denying divine existence.'

Cromwell answered, 'It doesn't work that way, you can be incinerated for being a Sacramentarian and denying the effectiveness of either the English or Catholic mass but oddly enough you cannot be executed in England for denying God; the law has not yet caught up with the word 'atheism'. There are not enough of them to make it worthwhile. Don't be disturbed by our dinner party. It was more a schoolboy's bull session than a sensible adult conversation; the airing of ideas that are rarely thought about but seem exciting in their defiance. In the cold light of day our words sound silly, unsatisfactory and juvenile. We individually and collectively need an active and judging God in our lives. Otherwise all is disorder and cast in doubt. Can you imagine the royal supremacy without the endorsement of a willing God with the authority to command all subjects to obey; can you conceive of a Henry VIII divested of his divinity and acting simply as a common man? Not a single person at that dinner party would have described himself as an atheist. What I am is a self-made man absolutely loyal to my sovereign who speaks on earth for God. We all know which side our bread is buttered on, and we are content.'

'My difficulty, Thomas, is that I too am a self-made man, trained almost from birth to be a painter. There was no time for or interest in theology and philosophy. I know nothing about the ultimate meaning of existence or God's role in the saga of creation. I paint what I can see and feel. You can't paint God's purpose or the meaning of existence, just as you can't paint good order and social harmony. We have words to describe them but they lack substance to visually depict them. I prefer the reformed faith because it allows me to think and judge as I like, using the words and stories of the Bible as my guide. The biblical tales and personalities are easily translated into paint.'

'I wouldn't be too sure about your "Reformed faith",' warned Cromwell, 'any faith, claiming the absolute truth, will not ultimately be a friend to private thought and let you read the Bible as you please.'

'That may indeed be so. The Swiss Cantons where my wife and children live are already growing more and more intolerant of the likes of me. A more immediate problem, however, is my lack of knowledge of how man interprets God's purpose or the meaning in the universe. You remember that I kept silent most of the evening because I barely understood a word said. Can you enlighten me?'

'You want a course on cosmology? Life is too short,' laughed Wyatt.

'Not at all,' said Cromwell. 'Your trouble, Wyatt, is that you do not know how to simplify a subject. Allow me to give our friend a brief description of God's purpose. It may sound arrogant but I can simplify and summarise anything.'

'No wonder you are so popular with the king,' joked Wyatt.

Cromwell began his lecture by assuring Hans that the cosmos was tidy, ordered and emotionally satisfying. 'It makes sense, every part fitting together to form a universe in which God is the playwright, stage manager, director and producer. The observable universe is better mapped than most of man's terrestrial orb. It consists of a series of eleven transparent, crystalline spheres forever circling the earth, the focal and only stationary point of the universe. The eleven spheres organise and order all the things you hear men talking about: the four elements – earth, water, air and fire – circle the earth metaphorically; the sun, moon and five planets, plus another sphere for the fixed stars, all orbit the earth in majestic progression every twenty-four hours. Beyond human view or understanding are two more spheres, the primus mobile which, though motionless itself, imbues the entire system with the necessary drive and desire to sustain its twenty-four-hour daily march about the earth, and the final orb or sphere, the abode of God and the mansion of the angels in all their multitude, exists beyond time, space, and imagination; as you say, quite unreproducible and un-paintable. Everyone knows that out there in the firmament resides the ultimate truth about creation and the meaning of existence, be it a butterfly or the Bishop of Rome. Are you following me?'

Without giving his pupil time to reply, Cromwell continued. 'This universe, as you are forever being told, is the stage on which men and women enact the drama of salvation and damnation, choosing either good or evil, heaven or hell. Every event from the appearance of comets in the heavens to the destruction of hailstones and the sickness of disease and ill health are preordained and betoken God's purpose in which the soldiers of God are forever clashing with the regiments of Satan.

'The macrocosm and the microcosm of existence are meshed into a divine web ranging from the mindless rock underfoot and the soulless grasshopper to God himself. All things in heaven and earth are linked in what is called the "great chain of being". There is a kind of ladder of existence in the universe's tripartite unity – moral, physical and spiritual. From the most sublime seraph guarding the gates of the Most High through the various grades of celestial being in heaven to the humblest living organism and the basest piece of matter on Earth, God's plenitude is ordered by a hierarchy of innate nobility that guarantees the rule of degree, priority and place throughout the cosmos. It is an indisputable astrological, as well as moral, fact that "among the heavenly bodies the nobler orbs are raised highest". Fire, being the purest element, holds chief place; in the animal kingdom, the lion is king of beasts, the eagle the prince of the skies; the oak is the prince of the forests, the rose queen of flowers and the diamond the most valued gem. God, it is said, "set degree and estate in all His glorious works", an arrangement beginning at the most inferior or base and ascending upward according to the merit or estimation of the thing that is order. In short, the closer to God, the purer and the better.'

Here the Principal Secretary took breath and ceased his discourse. Wyatt took advantage of the silence and said, 'You are a veritable Thomas Aquinas, the master of summary and simplicity, but what about the political implications. What you say is philosophical whimsy unless you link it to the realities of political science. Do you know, Master Holbein, the connection between Cromwell's words and the existence of the political world in which we all are forced to dwell? God created not only a hierarchy of archangels and angels, not to mention fallen angels like Lucifer and Mephistopheles, but He also appointed on earth kings, princes and all other governors, all in good and necessary order. In fact, all things stand by order for without order nothing can exist. We are born by order, live by order and by order we make our end. By an order the carpenter hath his square, his rule and his plummet. Everyone, according to his station in the world, frames his life by an order decreed either by God or inherent in his social status.

'The State is a living organism of obedient and right-minded people who live together in concord and Christian love, in what preachers and theorists love to describe as the 'body politic', consisting of the heart, head and feet. The heart is the prince. As all wit, reason and sense comes from the heart, so springs all laws, power, order, justice and virtue from the king. The head is likened to the natural leaders of society, the aristocracy, gentry and clergy. The hands are the artisans, warriors and merchants, and the feet belong to the ploughmen and tillers of the soil whose labour sustains the rest of society. When each segment of the body politic knows its proper place and function, the whole society is healthy, happy and secure.'

Holbein broke into Wyatt's wordy and none-too-brief analysis of Tudor society to assure his lecturer that he had heard more times than he needed from preachers and potentates the need for obedience which he thought the self-centred creed of the aristocracy. 'I am a little surprised, masters Cromwell and Wyatt, to hear such words about the harmonious body politic spoken by commoners and sensible men as yourselves. Are you trying to educate me or indoctrinate me? At least what you describe is paintable. My life has been a continuous series of portraits of the political elite; that is why I was so delighted to give *The Ambassadors* its death's-head and a message greater than the mere depiction of their foolish accomplishments and reputation in life.'

As Wyatt and Cromwell left the building the Principal Secretary whispered to his friend, 'You underestimated and insulted the poor man; we must make recompense.'

§

They left the building together but parted company as they approached Whitehall, Wyatt going on to the palace, Cromwell ducking into an out-of-the-way tavern known for its excellent food and drink and its odd assortment of customers, both men and women. As he found himself a dark corner where it would be unlikely that he would be recognised, Cromwell spotted Jane Parker, Lord Rochford's wife, sitting alone at a table with what looked like a pack of cards laid out before her. He went over and sat down beside her. 'I am surprised to find you alone here, Lady Rochford, allow me to order you a tumbler of mead or ale. What is it that you are doing with the playing cards?'

'Welcome Master Cromwell, you catch me seeking privacy to practice with these Tarot cards. You know of them. A tumbler of mead would be pleasant.'

'Tarot cards, they must be fresh from Italy. Are you telling the future with them?'

'Yes and no, for I am no expert and am only practising. Shall I try to predict the future? Give me a name, and I will do my amateur best.'

'Try the queen, Anne Boleyn.' Jane looked at the Principal Secretary oddly, smiled and began to lay out the cards face down. Four cards in a row, then another row of four cards until she had a perfect square of four rows. 'Now, Master Secretary, turn up any three cards.' Cromwell did so, revealing first the hangman, suspended upside down by one foot, the other leg crossed in front of the vertical limb and the hair of his head tied to the bottom of the gallows. The second card picked was death, a skeleton with the sockets of its eyes covered by a blindfold. Thirdly, came a seated devil with two chained and naked ladies standing before him. She studied the cards, muttering, 'Oh my, Oh my' to herself. 'Christ Almighty, Master Cromwell, if I am correct, this a dreadful message. The future looks worse than troubled. The queen will die before the year is finished. She is a crowned falcon and has only six months to live.'

'How will she die?' asked Crowell in a mocking tone.

'By the sword!'

'Don't you mean axe?'

'No, I said sword.'

Cromwell looked long and hard at Jane in her black cloak and heavy veil that made her look more like a Muslim lady in purdah than an English matron. 'Are you then predicting civil war in England?'

'Not I, I say nothing. The cards alone speak.'

'Is this your wishful thinking or God's will?'

'It is difficult to know, but not even a witch can change God's decree.'

'You are wise to say so. Otherwise I might place you in the Tower to test your witch's powers.' The Principal Secretary continued to stare at Lady Rochford. He then visibly shrugged his shoulders and thought to himself that it was quite impossible that the fate of the kingdom could be known and predicted by the likes of this disagreeable old woman. 'Good day Lady Rochford. Your table is a little too exposed for my tastes.' Cromwell rose and returned to the dark corner from which he had come, ordered ale with a chunk of cheese, and began to contemplate his meeting with Holbein and now his strange encounter with Jane Parker. He was beginning to realise just how dangerous Jane could be.

CHAPTER VI

Killing the Falcon

Henry was standing in his bedchamber bleakly wondering what the New Year of 1536 would bring – for it had to be better than the last, with the worst harvest in eight years, virulent plague, religious strife, a new and highly militant pope set upon punishing England, and at home a divided policy between the pro-French and pro-Imperial interests – when he was handed a slip of parchment announcing the death of the Dowager Princess of Wales, his faux wife, Katherine of Aragon. He found himself deeply ambivalent about the news, oddly saddened but also feeling like dancing with joy; it was the end of a very unpleasant era in a way that his marriage to Anne had never been. Katherine had been an incredibly tiresome and stubborn old woman who precipitated a religious and constitutional revolution by her refusing to accept the political necessity of retiring quietly into a nunnery and allowing him to marry a younger woman who could give him a male heir to the throne. It was, he guessed, her overwhelming sense of Spanish lineage and pride. She could never imagine herself simply as a dynastic tool to further the Tudor bloodline and secure the succession. Katherine was a princess in her own right of two royal houses – Aragon and Castile – and she believed her child had purer blood than any Tudor king. Her death was a great relief – it got the Emperor Charles off his diplomatic back and the two countries could rebuild their friendly relations. Anne, who had been quite willing to murder her rival queen, would be delighted; and the child she was now carrying would be without a doubt a boy and undisputed heir to the crown. He hoped the news would make her pregnancy easier.

When Anne heard of her rival's death she was lying on her bed thinking of Jane Seymour, her husband's most recent partner in the endless pageantry of courtly love in which she could not participate in her present condition. Not a particularly sexy or good-looking woman but nevertheless a dynastic threat. She felt a surge of jealousy sweep over her; it was like no other shock of emotional turmoil she had ever experienced, a green-eyed monster with teeth dripping blood. 'The bitch wants my place on the throne next to Henry,' she thought, 'and only this growing bundle of life that I am carrying can protect me from her intrigues. God, how I hate her!' She delighted in the story of Jane's father who, as the story was told, had raped his daughter-in-law many times over and had at least one child by her. His son, Sir Edward Seymour of the king's privy chamber, when he learned of his father's lustful obsession, disowned both his children on the grounds that they had been sired by his father, annulled his marriage, jailed his wife in a nunnery and remarried. Imagine Henry marrying the daughter of such a family!

Katherine's death changed her dark mood in an instant. 'One down and two to go,' she laughed. 'It would be far sweeter if the Lady Mary and Jane Seymour were also both dead.' She got out of bed and did a little celebratory jig and scribbled a note to the king: 'The old cow is dead, the new calf is a third grown. I plan to wear the brightest yellow gown I possess, and arrange a dance in my chambers to display my happiness at the witch's demise. Please come to the dance.' Henry was at Whitehall because Parliament was closing out its business and the king and Cromwell were anxious to persuade it to restore to the crown its feudal dues, and Anne was in Greenwich. His Majesty wrote back that he would not wear yellow but a more sombre colour, and that he had to arrange for an appropriate funeral at Peterborough Cathedral for Katherine. He was bothered by the rumour that she had been poisoned but he knew that she had been sick to the point of dying for over two months.

§

As part of the Shrovetide festivities just before Lent and the joyous mood that had flooded the court at

Katherine's death, Henry planned a magnificent joust in which he expected to be the prime rider. His opponent was Richard Cromwell, Thomas's adopted son and blood nephew; it was a mark of great egalitarianism that a commoner had been elected to tilt against the king. It was the least Henry could do to celebrate the forthcoming arrival of a son whose mother by birth was also a commoner. The horses, divided by a wooden barrier, had started magnificently, thundering down the course, ablaze with heraldic colours and insignias. Both riders carried lances wedged tightly under their armpits and aimed at their opponents' heads. Each wore a hundredweight of protective armour, and Henry's bodily weight added another 250 pounds to what his horse was carrying at full gallop. Half way down the track, his steed tripped, faltered and began to fall, Henry fell off to the side, and the beast landed on top of him. His Majesty was unconscious for two hours and everyone thought him dead.

Cromwell was in a state; his son might be accused of killing the king. He rushed out into the course along with a half-dozen panicky colleagues, removed the king's helmet and peered down at eyes he was terrified would never again open. He tried to image Henry's death, what it would mean to him, to the religious revolution he was managing and to the succession to the throne that would be fought over by the religious and dynastic followers of the Lady Mary and the baby Elizabeth. He hoped Queen Anne by giving birth to a boy child would resolve the conflict. Sweat induced by fear and shock trickled down his face, and he whispered to himself, 'Maybe now is the time for me to flee the country and thwart my enemies' efforts to string me up like a butchered hog.' Out loud, he ordered four of the strongest men, helplessly trying to attend the king, to carry the heavy sovereign to the nearest tent, and ordered that Dr Butt be notified. Possibly he could perform the miracle of renewed life. The doctor strongly urged that the king's massive body not be moved into the palace despite the cold of the tent. 'His chest is moving ever so slightly,' he observed, 'so he is not dead but he might have sustained a severe concussion and moving him could be dangerous. I see no head injury but to be on the safe side I advise swabbing his head with walnut paste. I keep all sorts of medicines and remedies in my chambers in the palace.'

'What will walnuts do for his head?' asked Cromwell. Dr Butt looked at him as if he were a wayward and ignorant child. 'The kernel of a walnut, as you well know, looks in miniature exactly like the human brain, same shape and colouring, therefore it corresponds to the brain and is regarded by the medical world as the best cure for head wounds, headaches and concussions.' Cromwell offered to go to the doctor's rooms to get the paste. 'At least,' he thought, 'walnuts can't do the king any harm and it gives me something to do.'

On his return he found Henry exactly as he had left him, pale and comatose. Again his mind allowed in the awful thought of the king's death, and Thomas remembered what he had been told once about Anglo-Saxon law and its ancient definition of murder. If a host invited a friend to dinner and the friend was killed en route to his house by highway robbers or accident, the host was responsible because his invitation had started the chain of events that ended in his friend's death. 'Could,' his mind queried, 'the same principle be applied to my son Richard? Henry was crashing down the course bent on unseating him. He was the target and therefore the agent of the king's death. Emotions would be running high; indeed they were already running high, and a scapegoat would have to be found – his son Richard would make a perfect candidate.' Just as this horrible thought began to take form in Cromwell's mind, the king's eyes opened and he blinked. Slowly his mouth opened and he began taking deep gulps of air. 'Where am I? What happened?' The king's voice sounded weak and nasally.

'Your horse stumbled and fell with you underneath it. You are in one of the jousting tents,' Cromwell almost shouted in relief.

'Get me out of here. It's bloody cold,' the voice croaked. Cromwell ordered a chair litter and the king was carried back to the palace and his bedchamber where a blazing fire warmed the room. The king was helped into bed, where he signalled his Principal Secretary to come and sit beside him. 'This is just between the two of us,' he whispered, 'but I spoke to God!'

'You what?'

'You heard me, I spoke to God.'

'And what did He say?'

'That I would soon hear a terrible truth.'

'Can the truth ever be terrible? What did He mean? He wasn't joking, was He?'

'I am sure He wasn't but I couldn't see His face, only feel His presence, which was absolutely devastating, greater than any I have ever encountered even as a small boy.'

'Was God's voice male?'

'Of course, it couldn't have been female.'

'Sorry, I thought it might have been epicene, an "it", representing both sexes.'

'Well, my God is not an "it". He is masculine through and through. What am I supposed to do about this forthcoming truth?'

Cromwell thought a minute and said, 'I would do nothing and tell no one.'

'Why? Because I can't handle the truth?'

'No. You can handle anything, Your Majesty. It is everyone else I worry about.' He looked over at the king and discovered that he had gone to sleep. 'Best cure for him,' thought the Principal Secretary.

Anne was surrounded by her ladies in waiting who crowded around her. Five days had passed since hearing of the king's tilting accident. 'I feel quite unwell,' she complained. 'I can't be sure what is wrong. Maybe I need a chamber pot. Get me to bed. You, Mary, stay; the rest of you be gone.' She had already started to bleed, had pelvic pains and a dull backache, all awful signs that God had forsaken her and her child was about to leave her. Her sister got her to bed and three hours later a fifteen-week-old foetus arrived in the midst of a blast of terrible pain and a flow of blood. Anne felt totally emptied; there was nothing left except a sense of utter exhaustion and deep depression. She was useless as a queen and as a woman. Despite the ordeal and terrible loss, Mary Boleyn thought that Anne had been rather lucky given the quickness of the event; that is if luck had anything to do with pain and suffering. It was always safer to say God's will was responsible for what happened. Miscarriages could often last two or more days, not three hours, and the foetus had been whole, no bits and pieces left behind to fester, poison and bring on death.

After cleaning up her sister Mary notified Anne's ladies in waiting what had happened and wondered who should tell the king. Probably Jane Parker, Lady Rochford, she thought, would do it. She always liked to be the bearer of bad news and analyse the reaction. She hoped there would be sufficient delay so that the queen could get a little rest.

Henry was on horseback when he received the news. He had been out hunting and had just returned when Jane Parker came rushing out the main entrance of Greenwich Palace – she must have ridden madly from Whitehall to get here – and waved him down. He heard her report, his ruddy colouring turning a leaden white. He said nothing except bid his company to stay where it was, turned his mount and trotted off toward from whence he had come. He needed to be alone.

In the quiet of the forest he sat pleading with God. Why had the Lord done this to him? What had he done to deserve the destruction of everything he had sacrificed so much for, worked so hard for? Was it too much to ask for a son to secure the succession for the good of the kingdom? What and whom had brought this calamity about? Endless questions and no answers.

Cromwell rode up beside him and asked whether he could help in any way. Henry replied by asking the question uppermost in his mind: 'Is this the 'terrible truth' that God warned me about?'

'No, Your Majesty, I am quite sure it is not. This is the queen's second miscarriage within little more than a year. The first misadventure came twelve months before you spoke to the Lord. If God made no mention of the first why should He turn her second miscarriage into a terrible truth? It happens all the time. My late wife had a miscarriage before my son Gregory was finally born.'

'Well, when will it be revealed?'

'We can only wait and see. Knowing God it will happen when we least expect it.'

'You blaspheme the Lord, Thomas; a dangerous thing to do. I suppose I must go and speak to her.'

'Do you want me to accompany you, Sir?'

'Yes, that might be helpful.' They rode back to Greenwich to find a barge to row them upstream to Whitehall and the stricken queen.

They arrived to find Anne in bed looking pale and worn; she had aged a decade since the king had last seen her, wrinkles around the eyes and neck, a sagging double chin and mottled complexion. The expression on her face, however, said that she was ready to fight God and the king to assign blame for what had happened. As soon as Anne saw Henry, she exclaimed, 'This is your fault! You almost scared my baby out of me by your fall during the joust. They told me you might be dead. I could almost hear our son scream. Then my ladies told me that dull bunch of lard, Jane Seymour, was with you at Greenwich sitting on your lap. Little wonder that I miscarried from shock and worry. Our child refused to live in such a world.'

Henry was mute in the face of such a barrage of words, but finally broke in and said, 'You know perfectly well that Jane sitting on my lap meant nothing; it was only a silly manifestation of courtly love and ritual that occurs regularly. As for how you were told of my tilting accident, that was old Norfolk being his usual clumsy self, a bull in an apothecary shop. You must rest, Sweetheart, and get well.'

Anne brushed aside the king's efforts to preserve the peace, and continued her tirade, 'I also know that you sent that well-trained bitch with the father that sired his own grandchildren a bag full of money and a letter inviting her into your bed. Somebody wisely warned her to return the money, leave the letter unopened, and to request you not to approach her until she had made a respectable marriage. And now you think the puppet a model of decorum and girlish modesty.'

'Anne, you are being difficult again. Katherine never carried on like this even after four miscarriages and a still birth.'

'Of course, she wouldn't. She never loved you the way I do. She married you for business and dynastic reasons, not for love. She knew the rules of the game: fornicate with her husband, manage his household and do his laundry but otherwise leave his sex life alone.'

'That not true, Anne, I knew Katherine for five years before we were married and I was deeply fond of her. Right now I think she was a hell of lot easier to live with than you.'

'Oh she was, was she, like when she refused to retire into a nunnery or give you an annulment of your marriage? Some quiet, dutiful wife Katherine was, more a martyr than a consort. As for your precious fondness, Henry, fondness is not love. Don't you remember how we both felt in those early days when we were courting and making love? We were ready to defy all of Christendom and wage war against the holiness of the Pope to marry and conceive a child. And yes, your fondling Jane Seymour's breasts turns me green with jealousy.' She burst into tears and buried her face in the pillows. Neither Henry nor Cromwell could think of anything to say, and they slipped quietly out of the room. 'God,' he whispered, 'what a wild horse she is. Why do I still love her?'

'Enough,' Cromwell asked, 'to defy Christendom once again?'

'All things wane a little over the course of time,' the king answered.

'Do you think your marriage defective?' Cromwell asked.

'It's hard to say. The similarities to my first marriage are startling: in both cases useless baby girls – Mary and Elizabeth – then miscarriages, stillbirths and children too frail to live. Leviticus's warning that marriage to my brother's wife would make me childless was a terrible revelation. I wonder what will be revealed to me about my marriage to Anne?'

§

Anne sat on the edge of her immense four-poster bed; Jane Parker, Lady Rochford, sat on a stool next to the bed. The two women were deep in a conversation that could be carried on nowhere else. Anne went to the root of the matter: 'My miscarriage was well over a month ago; I must think about getting pregnant again; my life depends upon it. You, Jane, have potions, magic spells and incantations, help me.'

'Possibly, but don't you need a man to do the job?' Jane answered.

'Of course, but I am responsible for the miscarriages. I simply can't risk another,' bemoaned Anne.

'You are sure of that responsibility?'

'What do you mean?' asked Anne.

'Well,' said Jane, 'it might be worthwhile to think about two wives and their patterns.'

'I don't follow.'

'The late queen and yourself,' Jane explained, 'you both had a series of miscarriages or stillborn children. Were you both responsible or was someone else?'

'Kindly do not refer to Katherine as the late queen. She was the Dowager Princess of Wales, Arthur's widow. What do you mean by someone else? You can't be referring to Henry?' Anne stated with shock.

'I most certainly am. Mark my words; another pregnancy by the king will end in another miscarriage. Remember, the dowager princess had six pregnancies, her daughter Mary and five dead children. You had two miscarriages following the birth of the Princess Elizabeth. Henry was the father of all nine. There must be something wrong with his seed.'

'What could possibly be wrong with his sperm?' asked Anne. 'True, occasionally he has trouble getting his instrument to stand up and bark but most of the time he is as lusty as any other man although his equipment is somewhat small for such a hulk of a husband.'

'I don't know the medical or spiritual reasons; all I am asking you is to think about the pattern – one child per wife, then after that nothing but dead children.'

'So you think my husband is responsible for my inability to carry a child to term? If that is true, then I am totally undone,' cried Anne.

'There is another option … find another man. The male sperm is unrecognisable.'

'Good God Almighty, Jane, you are speaking treason!' A long pause ensued. 'Who would dare such a thing?'

'What about one of the king's gentlemen of the bed chamber?' suggested Jane. 'Pick a stud who can perform.'

'And how do I do that?' asked Anne beginning to accept the possibilities of Jane's suggestion.

'Compare anatomy.'

'I think I know what you are saying. So let us go down the list of the king's gentlemen who regularly visit my chambers. There is my brother George. But he is out of the running. Mating with him would be incest.'

'He is horny enough, and well enough endowed to overcome any obstacle. I wouldn't put it past him.' Jane stated with a scowl.

'Don't let your hatred toward and disappointment in George blind your good sense. What about Thomas Wyatt? He is certainly eligible and has two children to prove his worth. I have first-hand knowledge; his equipment is rather small, although his technique is excellent. The trouble with Thomas is that the king is already a little suspicious of him. No, he is too dangerous.'

'There are William Brereton and Henry Norris.'

'William is far too old; it would be like sleeping with your father. Henry is certainly a possibility but I suspect he is too loyal to the king, and possibly to me, to sire a faux heir to the throne. What about Mark Smeaton? Yes, he is a real possibility. It is very amusing to think of the future King of England being the grandson of a Flemish carpenter. And I am pretty sure I know how to get a look at his mating apparatus. Jane, go and fetch the singing man, and we will see how well he performs. Be sure, Jane, to supply me with an aphrodisiac potion to put in the king's wine; that will keep him coming to my bed and prevent anyone thinking in terms of a substitute father or faux son.'

Lady Rochford returned with Smeaton in tow. She had found him in his room practising on his lute. Her Majesty ordered Jane out of her chamber and told Mark to stand by her bed. 'This,' she said, 'is the only really private spot in my entire section of the palace. How have you been, Mark?'

'Since the last time I saw you, Your Highness, was last evening, I confess to being the same as before.'

'Actually I was being nostalgic and was wondering about the first time we met, when I insulted your voice and manhood. It is a little late but I wanted to apologise. Your voice certainly was croaking but I had no first-hand knowledge of your sexual equipment or even hearsay information to disparage it. I simply made up the smallness of your stones. I want to correct what I am sure was an error, and inspect them for myself.' As she spoke she got off the bed and undid the ties holding Mark's codpiece in place. 'I hope you don't mind my taking a peak.' She reached her hand in to his codpiece and grabbed Mark's balls and pecker and brought them out into the daylight. His penis immediately started to engorge.

Mark stood there with a shocked expression on his face mixed with a smile and said, 'Your Highness may have difficulty getting Roger back into his cave. There is no longer enough room.'

'That is easily remedied even though Roger has grown to an impressive size.' She leaned down and took the throbbing penis in her mouth, began to suck and run her tongue along its length and head. Mark stood there, his entire body started to tremble, and he seized one of the nearest posts of the bed to hang on for dear life. When he had come to climax, the queen tucked his genitals back into his codpiece and neatly tied up his ribbons. Then she walked over to a potted plant on a table and daintily spat into it and washed her mouth out with white wine. 'I couldn't,' she laughed, 'tell from the expression on your face whether you were more shocked or satisfied, but at the very least you can now boast that you had fellatio with a queen. Sit down on this stool. I need to talk to you. You fit my every need. You are a strapping young man in every respect and I need you to do me a favour. I need a partner to take the king's place and make an heir to the throne.'

'You are joking, of course.'

'No! Certainly not. I am deadly serious.

'Possibly a queen might escape, but I would be dead, most unpleasantly, if I did as you suggest.'

'Don't be silly, there is no danger to either of us. I have arranged for Lady Rochford to collect you at night after everyone has gone to bed. She will know when I am at the most fertile. You can undress in the spice and jam room – we call it the marmalade closet – and then come creeping naked to my bed every time I call for marmalade. We cannot risk your leaving a piece of male clothing in by bedchamber.'

'Your Highness, I beg of you, your plan is far, far too dangerous, especially allowing Lady Rochford to orchestrate the affair. You know she was arrested and taken in custody at Greenwich last week for rioting with a bunch of women in favour of Katherine's daughter, the Lady Mary. She can't be trusted, nor can I.'

'I know all about Jane's arrest. It was all a mistake, and it was simply bad timing that she stepped outside for a walk when the pro-Mary crowd was gathering, and she got swept up in it. As for not trusting you, I could tell that you vastly enjoyed my little example of forthcoming pleasures; when we seriously join forces and do the real thing, there will be no doubt in your mind. Moreover, I can always call the whole adventure off, complain to the king that you have been deliberately neglecting me, and you will be fired and out on the street without a job or recommendation. That is the consequences of failure to cooperate and obey your queen!'

With the risk to his determination to become a gentleman and the irony that this woman who had so humiliated him now wished to use his common-born seed, Smeaton realised he had no other choice except to say, 'Yes, I will be ready whenever you call.'

§

Smeaton and Cromwell were walking in the king's private garden enjoying the spring sunlight and watching a myriad of small clouds scurry across a blue sky. 'The queen has been in a frenzy ever since her miscarriage,' Mark told Thomas, 'as if she were trying to cram a lifetime into a fortnight. I sing, play the lute and virginal for her and her company almost every night, and she conducts a salon in the French fashion, wine, dancing, and laughter, with her maids vanishing late at night into the closets and rooms where the supplies and spices are stored for a little romp with the gentlemen of the king's chambers. Lots of fun and giggling. The gentleman of the chambers take over the place – George Boleyn and Francis Weston are the horniest but Wyatt and Richard Page aren't far behind. Brereton acts his age, he is over fifty, and sticks to wine and song, and Sir Henry Norton mops lovelorn about the rooms wishing he had Anne to himself. They have known and liked one another for over a decade.'

'How long have these antics been going on?'

'They began over a year ago when the king developed an interest in Madge Shelton, Anne's cousin. The queen was outraged, even talked about having the poor girl expelled from court, and began to hold more and more frantic soirees in her chambers, possibly hoping to recapture her husband's flagging attentions.'

'Speaking of capturing, I thought Elizabeth Browne, the Countess of Worcester, rather on the plump side when last I saw her. Has she been sleeping around and if so with whom? Not you, I hope; she is too occupied with sports for the likes of you.'

'You are right, she's not my type, and she has put on weight. The word is that Francis Weston is responsible; his mind is rarely off of the equipment that dangles between his legs, and I can readily imagine the two of them turning the lush grasses of the bowling green or the leafy bowers of the forests into lovers' beds for their mating. For myself I much prefer a four-poster bed.'

As they spoke the lady in question came rushing down a palace corridor trying to avoid notice by her brother, Sir Anthony Browne of the king's chamber. Sir Anthony had picked up rumours that his sister may be pregnant and wanted to check for himself, especially since her husband had been on diplomatic mission to the merchants of the Hanseatic League in Germany.

'Elizabeth! Please stop. I need to talk to you.' With nowhere to hide, Lady Worcester did as she was ordered, turned and sweetly said, 'Anthony, what do you want?'

Sir Anthony inspected his sister with a discerning eye and bluntly said, 'Are you *enceinte*, Elizabeth?'

'What makes you think that?'

'Because I have had six children and can tell the difference between a few pounds of over-indulgence and a child in your belly. How did it happen and who is responsible?'

'I am not sure,' Elizabeth replied weakly.

'Not sure!' Anthony responded angrily. 'Does that mean you have been sleeping around?'

'Not exactly. Francis Weston is the most likely candidate, but it could also be my husband's.'

'What will Worcester say to a strange bun in his oven?'

'It's my oven, not his, and he is in no position to complain. He "sleeps around" all over Europe and England.'

Sir Anthony was aghast and deeply shocked at his sister's cavalier attitude towards her sexual activities and upbraided her for dishonouring the family name and acquiring the reputation of a common whore. In her turn Elizabeth was equally angered by her brother's words and struck back by exclaiming, 'You disparage a small fault in me, while overlooking a much greater sin that is far more damaging. Don't you know what regularly goes on in the queen's chambers? And I am not just talking about Bessie Holland, one of Her Highness's more wayward ladies in waiting, who has been the Duke of Norfolk's mistress for years. I am talking about Mark Smeaton dipping his wick into the queen on a regular basis. Then there is the queen's brother, Viscount Rochford, who comes to visit late at night in his sleeping gown. It is easy enough to guess what they are up to.' Elizabeth was so agitated that she began naming other members of the queen's chambers.

As the sister grew more and more frenzied and vocal, the brother became more and more silent realising the awful predicament his sister had unwittingly put him. He was duty bound to inform the king – if he failed to do so and the truth became common knowledge, he could be accused of treasonously concealing the queen's adultery. But to report the queen's behaviour and discover that the story was false could also be treasonous for having slandered the queen. He was between a rock and the proverbial hard place.

After he left his sister, Anthony discussed the matter with two other gentlemen of the king's chambers and together with beating hearts and trembling legs they informed Henry, but their version of Elizabeth Browne's accusations were seriously broadened in the telling: 'Your Majesty, when at night you retire, the queen has a series of sexual minions already lined up. Her brother is by no means last in queue. Sir Henry Norris and Mark Smeaton would not deny that they have spent many nights with her without having to persuade her, for she herself urged them on and invited them with presents and caresses.'

Henry listened carefully to his gentlemen of the chamber. He knew that his court was crawling with rumours, especially about the queen, and he was darkly sceptical. He refused to be stampeded into senseless action on the basis of sheer rumours voiced by panicky women. Nonetheless, he ordered Cromwell to make a full and immediate inquiry.

Cromwell led Smeaton down a set of thirteenth-century stairs to the oldest part of the cellar of his renovated sixteenth-century home in Putney. The house had a new banqueting hall and modern kitchen and a fine walking gallery for exercise in cold and inclement weather. He still called his home Austin Friars, after its original monastic name. 'No one ever goes down here anymore except an occasional rat and lots of hard weaving spiders,' he told Mark.

'Then why are we?' asked Mark.

'Largely because you require me to do so.'

'I don't like the sound of those words, Thomas. You aren't jailing me in your basement like Sir Thomas More did to those suspected heretics?'

Cromwell unlocked a massive iron gate, put his torch in a metal ring on the wall, and they entered a large room with a heavy table, a three-legged stool and an uncomfortable-looking cot. There was a small barred window off to one side. 'You have it partly right. No one suspects you of heresy but your name has emerged in a case of adultery,' he explained. 'Sit down Mark and let's talk.'

As Mark perched on the stool, Cromwell began his questioning. Bluntly he asked, 'Have you been sleeping with the queen?'

Smeaton answer was to turn deadly white in the face and cry out, 'Oh God, help me!'

'Have you, yes or no?' demanded Cromwell.

Smeaton hesitated, but finally answered, 'I guess the truth is a little of both. I was ordered by the queen to mate with her, not out of lust but for reasons of State. Did that bitch Lady Rochford inform on me? I warned the queen she could not be trusted!'

'For reasons of State! Explain yourself.'

'The queen called me into her bedchamber and told me she needed a young, well-endowed surrogate father to sire a son; she was afraid that if she slept only with the king they would have yet another miscarriage. I naturally declined, and she said either I cooperate or be kicked out of her service without a recommendation and thus to live on the street. I had no choice; it was strictly a business proposition.'

Cromwell, a skilled interrogator, hid from his face and words the realisation that his friend had just openly confessed to high treason. Instead he conversationally asked, 'And what did you, Mark, get out of this business proposition?'

'I swear, nothing but to keep my position in the queen's household. I had only just afforded my new set of horses and my fancy livery for my servants.'

'How many times did you copulate?'

'Three; the Rochford bitch told me when Her Highness was most fertile and arranged our meeting.'

'How often did you come to climax?'

'Only once, the first time; I was too embarrassed to try a second time. But in the second and third sessions I stayed longer. She always treated me like a servant, never a gentleman, but in bed she accepted me as a man and a lover. I must admit, she was wonderfully exciting and compelling when naked between the sheets.'

'So enjoyment and lust conjoined with business and matters of State?' Cromwell asked, beginning to reveal the severity of his questioning.

'I guess so. What am I to do? You must help me, Thomas. Can we keep the whole thing quiet?'

'I am afraid not. Lady Worcester has already confessed to what has been going on the queen's chambers at night and actually named you as having slept with the queen. The king has been informed and has ordered a full investigation. The court is already awash with rumours about you and others. I will do my best, Mark, I owe you for my career, but this is all far too serious for me to make any promises. It is not just adultery, which, even with a queen, is not a capital offence, but you have admitted to treason, attempting to sire a fake king and manipulate the royal succession. That is almost the same as conspiring the king's death and you know the penalty for that.'

Mark Smeaton began to shrink visibly as he huddled on his stool, his entire body shaking.

Jane Parker, Lady Rochford, was announced; Cromwell rose from his seat and asked her what brought her ladyship to Austin Friars.

Without preamble, Jane stated her purpose: 'You have brought Mark Smeaton here; when are you going to send him to the Tower?'

'And why, Lady Rochford is this a matter of concern or interest to you, and why should I send him to the Tower?'

'Very little happens at the palace without my knowing about it. There can be only one reason why you whisked him off under guard to your house; he was caught impregnating the queen.'

'And what may you know about that?' the Principal Secretary coldly asked.

'I make most of the queen's private arrangements and I know exactly what is going on in her chambers.'

'Are you saying you are a procuress, supplying Her Majesty with male flesh? A dangerous occupation.'

'I only informed Smeaton when the queen wished to see him. I never stayed to find out why he answered my call.'

'Then how are you in a position to accuse either the queen or Smeaton of adultery?'

'Because I overheard them making plans to meet. I bet the young man has already broken down and told you. But actually, Master Secretary, that is not the reason I am here. I have quite a different tale to tell.'

'Please be brief. I have much to do.'

'Put as briefly as I can, my husband, Lord George Rochford, has been committing incest with his royal sister. Is that brief enough?'

Cromwell continued to eye the woman with ever-increasing distaste. 'Please continue.'

'All the ladies of the queen's chambers know that George appears regularly in Anne's bedroom dressed only in his sleeping robe with nothing on underneath it. They sit and chatter and laugh about the king, disparaging his verse, his dancing and his sexual expertise. Worse, there is familiarity between the queen and her brother beyond what so near a relationship could justify.'

'Are you saying that they actually fornicated in front of you?'

'Well no, but I have been in the bedchamber and could see kissing, and wrestling, their hips moving rhythmically under the blankets, but I never actually observed penetration.'

'Enough of this! You disgust me. Is your hatred for your husband so great that you are willing to bring the queen to the scaffold block?'

Jane was quiet for a long minute. Finally she whispered in a low, throaty voice: 'Anne Boleyn and I go back a long way. We met first at my marriage to George and then on a regular basis when I moved to Hever Castle as a member of the family. I offered her friendship; she gave back only distain. I performed black magic and alchemical miracles for her including when I destroyed the hated cardinal at her request, in return she would not even recognise me as a full member of the Boleyn family. My usefulness assured me a place first in the palace and then in her royal chambers but she never confided in me, always preferring her sister or that stupid bundle of sexual desires, the Countess of Worcester. I said nothing when she goaded the king into heresy and guaranteed the destruction of his soul by the wicked magic she used to blind him into marriage and crowning her queen. She deserves to die given what she did to good queen Katherine, trying to poison her and her daughter Mary, not to mention the destruction of the true religion. She is a vile whore, whom the tarot cards foretold would die horribly.'

'And what are you Mistress Parker, a noble and loyal servant of the king or a vengeance-seeking papist and occult-practising old hag? You claim to have destroyed Wolsey with your black arts. That was back in 1526; the cardinal did not die till 1530, four years later. Given another four years, pigs could have learned to fly. And as for the cards, that is simply more of your skullduggery.'

'You are not a believer, Master Secretary; don't ever underestimate Satan. The day may come when you could use my powers and I won't lift a finger to save you.'

§

Cromwell and Thomas Cranmer, the Archbishop of Canterbury, a wonderfully mellow man with a bland face but stubborn mouth, who abhorred controversy and was terrified of his king but on occasion could muster up enough courage to talk back to him, stood bareheaded before the king in his most private closet.

'All right, Master Secretary, tell me what you have learned about these egregious rumours swirling about the queen,' the king growled.

Cromwell cleared his throat and ran his hand through his thick hair. He could feel the sweat trickling down his forehead. 'There does seem to be evidence that the queen has been behaving in a dangerously silly fashion,' he murmured.

'Speak up man! In what silly fashion?'

'I have spoken to all the ladies of the chamber, in particular to Lady Worcester, who suggests that both Mark Smeaton and Sir Henry Norris have found their way under the queen's bedcovers. George Boleyn has been named by Lady Worcester and his own wife, Lady Rochford, as the queen's sex mate. William Brereton and Francis Weston have also been mentioned as a favourite of the queen's chambers, and so has Thomas Wyatt.'

'This is unbelievable.' Henry had turned a horrified white. 'My closest and longest friend, the groom of the stool and head of my privy chamber, has cuckolded me, my wife has betrayed and scorned me, and worse, she has found her own brother a better lover than her own husband. Cromwell, this is God's "terrible truth". There is absolutely no doubt in my mind. My wife is worse than a common trollop; she is an incestuous whore who seduces her own brother and her husband's best friend.'

'We have not interrogated those named in adultery and so far it is mostly hearsay except for Mark Smeaton's confession: he admits to sleeping with the queen three times.'

'Good God. She lusts for a commoner! She has either lost her mind or the devil has taken hold of her!'

'I am afraid, Sire, it is worse than that. She and Smeaton seem to have committed treason. She ordered him into her bed so that his seed might fertilise a healthy male infant unbeknownst to you, who would inherit the throne. She blames you, not herself, for all the miscarriages she has suffered.'

'This is appalling.' The king's complexion had turned from ghostly white to angry red. Yet he neither roared nor wept in rage and anguish. He whispered and trembled as if unable to comprehend his own words. 'Cromwell, God has spoken. He warned me, and now He has revealed the full frightfulness of her adultery and treason. This revelation is no accident; God knew this would happen, that Lucifer, Satan and Beelzebub would all three consume the queen in unspeakable sin. My marriage must be dissolved and the woman must burn for her crimes both to me as a man and to my majesty as a king. The kingdom will demand it, and so will God. I must protect what little I have left from this demon. She is quite capable of poisoning both my daughter, the Lady Mary, and my son, Henry Fitzroy. Have the queen and her paramours sent immediately to the Tower for interrogation and safekeeping, and bundle Smeaton off after them. Tell him he deserves as lingering and painful a traitor's death as the executor can devise. Go about your constabulary duties, Cromwell, but Cranmer stay with me for a while. I need a shoulder to cry on. I know you loved the woman, so we will cry together.'

'A word, please, Your Majesty. Mark Smeaton, whose music used to be lyrical to your ears, is more a victim than a criminal. The queen placed him in an impossible position. She threatened that if he did not perform satisfactorily in bed and his equipment stand erect, she would have him fired from her chambers and kicked out on the street without a recommendation.'

'He should have reported the conversation to me!'

'And would you have believed him? He really was inbetween Scylla and Charybdis and picked what he felt to be the lesser evil.'

'No,' the king countered, 'he picked by far the greater evil but thought it was the lesser cost. He was wrong! He will pay dearly for fucking the queen.' Cromwell had never heard him use that word before.

Once the Principal Secretary had left, Henry and his archbishop clung to one another. There was nothing to say. The abyss had opened up and Henry's world had fallen in. 'How could this have happened?' the king almost wept with frustration and dismay. 'Thomas, what is God's purpose in overwhelming me and my kingdom with this horror? What have I done to deserve such heartrending punishment?'

'Why do you blame yourself? Why not the devil?'

'It is either me or God; God possesses foreknowledge and could have prevented the devil's actions. Moreover, God warned me. He spoke to me during my jousting accident. Didn't Cromwell tell you?'

'No, Your Highness.'

'When I was unconscious He made His presence known. I didn't see Him but felt His unimaginable majesty. It was an extraordinary experience. You would have approved, Cranmer. You are forever telling me that God has no corporeal form and cannot be represented in visual shape and therefore all images of Him are both graven and idolatrous. Only the dullness of man's wit requires images and idols. God warned me that a terrible truth would be revealed, and now it has. Has the deity spoken to me because of the special office I hold? I am His faithful vassal and must discharge my responsibilities to divine authority being in the room that I am in. It is more important for me to do my duty than for any other human on earth. So, Thomas, what am I to do? This awful affair goes to the core of my belief in a Christian God.'

'If God really warned you, He will guide you. You must have faith. As you said earlier He has absolute foreknowledge. When we cannot understand God's intent there is nothing left except faith.'

'Mr Archbishop, are you questioning my word, the word of a divine right king? What do you mean by saying if God really spoke to me? Of course He did. I know the difference between a mere dream and a divine message. Quit doubting my word and spouting faith in God at me. My wife has been beset by the devil and has been swept up in treason. That is not a matter of faith; it is the triumph of evil. What I need to know is how do I tell the difference between what my personal conscience tells me and God's will?'

'You have been through this before, my liege, with the debate over the legality of your first marriage. You drove through your divorce in the face of almost universal European opposition and the threat of divine punishment and eternity in hell. You did so because God and your conscience told you that you were right. As you yourself put it, you knew you were right not because so many said it but because you knew the matter to be right. Don't forget you are a divine right sovereign.'

'True, true, though the law of every man's conscience be but a private court, yet it is the highest and supreme court for judgment or justice. I must now decide what I have done to bring God's wrath down upon me. I remember years ago that I once told the Venetian ambassador that I could not see that there is any faith in the world, save in me, and therefore God Almighty, who knows this, prospers my affairs.'

'That is certain, when we have faith we need no other thing more and the satisfaction of your sins cannot be achieved by simple-minded deed-doing.'

'Wrong, Cranmer, you know me well enough to realise that God's wrath can only be deflected by absolute obedience, every man doing that duty assigned him by his station in life. Faith in his mercy has very little to do with it. You know and I know that it is written in Leviticus for all to read that "if ye will not harken unto me, the Lord thy God, then I will appoint over you terror, consumption, and the burning ague and ye shall sow your seed in vain, and

I will break the pride of your power, and make your heaven as iron and earth as brass. And if you walk contrary unto me I will bring seven times more plague upon you according to your sins." If what happened today isn't seven times more plague than befalls the common man, I can't image what it is. As the Lord my God punishes me so I must punish those who have brought these terrible plagues and betrayals upon me. There can be no room for mercy or forgiveness. How can you say that I cannot understand God's design? I have spent a lifetime fulfilling His every command, never even allowing the hunt to interfere with His divine services; I regularly attend mass three times a day. How could I have taken on the responsibilities of Supreme Head of the Church of England without understanding God's intent?'

'I meant His ambitions for you personally, not His grand design for the universe. All I am saying is that when there is no good explanation or answer, then we must rely on faith. I can do nothing but grieve that the human mind and soul can harbour such thoughts that passed through the queen's mind, and pray that these events do not deter you from the spiritual revolution that you have begun, bringing your kingdom out of the misery, evil and thralldom of papal Catholicism.'

'No, Cranmer, I don't rely on faith. I look for the cause of the sin that God is punishing. My duty is to obey His laws and fulfil His severe and inflexible justice, not depend on faith in the existence of His capricious mercy. Christians are the inheritors of

God's kingdom but only if they preserve His precepts and laws, and do good works. I know, Thomas, that you at one time thought highly of the lady (as did I), and it was a blow to be told that she is a sinkpot of evil and must be destroyed. God commands it. Without such festering sin the future must improve, and I may well realise what has been the driving force of my life for the past ten years – a male heir.'

'You then have already chosen a new wife?'

'Mistress Jane Seymour must do.'

The Principal Secretary was sitting at his desk reading a letter that had just arrived from Sir William Kingston, the deputy governor of the Tower. He described Anne's dignified if ironic arrival by barge to Traitors' Gate on the river and then into the fortress itself at the Court Gate. Her presence in the Tower was signalled by a single blank cannon shot, a sad comparison to the thunderous barrage that had greeted her less than three years before at her coronation. Sir William reported that her composure held until the privy councillors, who had accompanied her, turned to return to Greenwich leaving her alone, penned behind terrifyingly thick stonewalls. She fell to her knees and burst into tears, then into wails mixed with frenzied laughter. Laughter had been her hallmark and her constant protector against the cruel vagaries of life. She had laughed at Mark Smeaton's humiliation and meagre testicles thirteen years past, at Wolsey's orders to evict her from court, at the Pope's many and footless threats of excommunication, at her husband's failure to stand erect and perform like a man, and again at Mark's silly fears that in inseminating her he was defying the sacred purity of royal blood. Laughter had been her prop and stay, making the trials of existence bearable. Now it was mixed with hysteria.

'Master Kingston,' she managed to cry out amidst tears and coughing, 'shall I go into a dungeon?'

'Certainly not, Madame, you shall go into lodgings that you lay in at your coronation. You are still a queen.'

'It is too good for me. Jesus, have mercy on me! Someone notify the king that a terrible mistake has been made and I must be rescued from my enemies.' Anger and the once bright spark of competition were beginning to re-emerge.

Cromwell kept on reading. Then he suddenly stopped, put down the letter, and said aloud 'Good God, this is unbelievable. Only God could have made her condemn herself in her own mouth. Richard,' he shouted, 'come here and read this!'

Richard Cromwell hastened to his father's call and was handed Kingston's letter, which he read, and said, 'Holy mother of God! Has she lost her mind?' He read aloud what the deputy had written. 'It is reported to me by the ladies, including my wife, who have been assigned to guard and attend the queen, that Anne had bragged about her encounter with Sir Henry Norris a week or so ago. I had heard rumours of it but this is a first-hand account from the queen herself. The queen was in her presence chamber when she began to berate Norris for having committed himself to marriage with Margaret Shelton, the queen's cousin and at one time probably Henry's bed partner, and then refusing to go through with it. Norris passed off the criticism with a joke, and the queen in anger said, 'You look for dead men's shoes; for if aught came to the king but good you would look to have me.' Norris, quite naturally, was horrified by these words and shouted that 'he would rather his head were off than fill royal shoes'. These words are appalling treason; she will burn for them. If, uncle, you wanted to destroy her, not just annul her marriage, here is your heaven-arranged chance.'

Cromwell took Kingston's explosive letter back and began to fold and refold it while he delayed answering his adopted son and blood nephew. 'No,' he finally said, 'I don't desire Anne's death by either the stake or the block. I simply want to do the king's bidding. But I grant you, her words are enough to stampede him into fierce action. If it rains it pours evidence of her misbehaviour. First we had her importing Smeaton into her bed as a surrogate father, now we have this! It is enough to make me believe in the current theological premise that there is no such thing as chance, coincidence and happenstance. God has foreknowledge of all things, has given divine purpose to all things, and what appears on the surface as bad luck and timing for the queen in having the serious scandals in her chamber revealed is in fact God's action, a warning and a revelation. The king already sees it in this fashion. He states he had a vision when he fell from his horse and was unconscious for two hours, that God spoke to him and forewarned him that he would soon suffer a "terrible truth". Now it has happened, and knowing His Majesty, nothing is going to change his mind that his wife deserves to die. I am not sure how much of all this I believe; God is always being hauled into the human equation. He is already sufficiently overburdened without being held responsible for Anne's death. You probably have noticed that I rarely gamble, I don't like pinning my life and career on either chance or God.

'Moreover, I am not convinced the queen's words were meant as treason. She loves to brag and overstate things. She is a master of verbal expression, using witty and rich words without regard to their meaning in common parlance. She can't describe the day as pleasant without adding a host of words and metaphors to enhance her words. She is saying in Kingston's letter no more than what is often stated, albeit always under one's breath, that the king is human and must die. Given his consumption of food, ale and wine, and his ever-increasing obesity, he will be lucky to last another decade. His leg is already ulcerated and a clot could kill him tomorrow. Granted, 'filling dead men's shoes' sounds dreadful, and the world will doubtless take it for treason, and it puts poor Norris in an terrible and probably fatal bind, but it is the same kind of silly and exaggerated statement as the Duke of Suffolk is always making. Like Anne, he speaks before he thinks … if he ever thinks. You remember his shouting out at the top of his lungs at the Blackfriars annulment trial that "England was well rid of cardinals", and Wolsey had to reprimand him. "Filling dead men's shoes" is on a par with the duke's ridiculous rantings. As for Norris waiting around to marry Anne once the king is dead, she does not say that she will be available to him either tomorrow or ten years from now. No, it was a stupid statement made in the passion of the moment and in language thrilling to Anne but horrifyingly treasonable to almost everyone else.'

In great surprise, Richard looked at his uncle and said, 'You seem to be defending the queen; I thought she was your sworn enemy and you needed to get rid of her and her Boleyn friends. Now is the perfect chance.'

Cromwell eyed his nephew and quietly said, 'Don't be so bloodthirsty. Anne is a political gnat. All you have to do is brush her off, not squash her and rub the bloody corpse into the ground. True, she has been a pest ever since the old queen died and the sore spot between the Emperor Charles and the king was removed and his family honour absolved. I have been weaning His Majesty into an Imperial alliance and friendship. Anne and the Boleyn party have been pressuring him to stay French in all things and join France against the emperor. With Anne's marriage annulled and the queen incarcerated in a nunnery she can do no more diplomatic harm. Rusticated from court she and her allies will no longer be able to protect the monasteries that the king and I have selected for destruction, their wealth going to fatten the royal exchequer to make the king per capita the wealthiest sovereign in Europe. Policy and politics will be much easier without her. She was constantly interfering and was incapable of being a proper royal wife, staying out of the way and birthing a bevy of royal heirs.'

'You almost sound as if you were not going to use her words at her trial,' a very perplexed Richard said.

'Oh! I will use them, be assured of that. They will be the lynchpin of the case, but if you give a little thought to the matter, they do not bear much weight at law. "Filling dead men shoes" was said to Lady Kingston and the other women under unknown circumstances. We do not have the full content of the conversation, only hearsay versions of the original. Her words may well have been tampered with to achieve treason. Those words were then told to Sir William who wrote them down, accurately we do not know, and sent them to me. In other words, the queen's remark has been twice edited and very likely improved by people who bear her no great love.'

'This I understand but what about Viscount Rochford, Norris, Weston and Brereton, not to mention Mark Smeaton, the helpless common lamb among the well-coated sheep. Are they guilty and must all die?'

'That is a somewhat different matter; a sense of balance is required. You can't have an adulterous queen without an appropriate number of fornicating admirers. To enjoy an omelette you must break a few eggs; how worthy they are remains to be seen.'

'But why isn't treason enough? Why must the queen also be accused of adultery?'

'Because in committing treason she slept with Smeaton and enjoyed every minute of their intercourse. That is adultery.'

§

'Today,' Cromwell meditated, 'is May the third, 1536; Smeaton was incarcerated and confessed on Sunday, April the thirtieth, and the queen and her hapless band of gentlemen of the king's chamber were imprisoned the following day. It is now time to talk at length to the gallant four and hear their versions of the truth and record their frantic claims to innocence.'

Sir Henry Norris walked into the interrogation chamber with studied nonchalance, his steps signalled neither reluctance nor artificial courage. The king's groom of the stool was at perfect ease either helping the king perform the most basic functions of life or talking to Cromwell about high treason and its dreadful consequences. He was the exquisitely polished man from the silver Saint Christopher medallion pinned to his bonnet to the Spanish leather boots that gleamed around his shapely legs. He stood before the Principal Secretary unruffled and courteous, for Norris made a fine art of politeness for all occasions, from thanking a scullery maid to flattering a duchess.

Cromwell was impressed; here was a true gentleman bred to the strictest standards of decorum. Nevertheless he came brutally without preamble to the point. 'Norris, did you really think you could outlive the king and thereby have his wife for your bedmate, or were you planning murder of God's anointed sovereign?'

'What on earth are you talking about?' Norris asked in outrage.

'I have the queen's own words that you look for "dead men's shoes and if aught came to the king you would have Mistress Anne for your own". I also have a host of witnesses that place you in the queen's bedchamber not even waiting for the king to die.'

'This is nonsense! The queen expressed herself badly. I said that I would rather lose my head than fill royal shoes. Do you honestly believe that I of all the king's gentlemen would forget what is more precious to me than life itself – my honour and my loyalty to my sovereign? I am not simply talking about myself but my entire family that has served kingship for four devoted generations. My great-grandfather served King Henry VI, the most saintly and perfect of monarchs; my grandfather waited upon Edward IV, my father was instrumental in bringing the first Tudor to the throne, and I regard the present king as my own brother.'

'You call Henry VI saintly; that is the huge difference between the two of us. I call the last of the Plantagenet monarchs the worst of kings, a fool and easily led figurehead who was responsible for the civil Wars of the Roses. His abdication and death were blessings. At heart, underneath all your fine gestures and gracious words, Norris, you are an antiquated medievalist, harking back to the horrors of the old days, which you call chivalric and saintly. I, in contrast, am a modern and self-fashioned man who needs neither family nor history to explain my success in life. If you really love the king as your brother, then understand his needs and position. He is a divine right monarch in direct communication with God, and divine insight has revealed to him the terrible truth about his queen. Her adultery is much more than a question of whether the king should dissolve his marriage and marry someone capable of providing him with an unimpeachable male heir. Her adultery and treason strike at the essence of his divinity. The speed and suddenness in which the evidence against the queen has fallen into our laps is clear proof to His Majesty that only God could have managed the revelation. Under the circumstances, I don't need a confession from you, Norris; your thoughts, which you cannot deny, are treasonous. Thoughts imply malicious intentions.'

'So now my thoughts are held to be criminal and will strip me of life and place me on the butcher block? I see no escape. Are you planning a mock trial and public bloodletting?'

'Protocol and ritual require a public hearing and ceremonial execution. But, even the great cardinal once said that "if the Crown were the prosecutor and asserted it, justice would be found to bring a verdict that Abel was the murderer of Cain".'

'God help us all' were Norris final words.

Francis Weston was next on Cromwell's list. He strode into the room as if ready for hand-to-hand combat with the king's secretary, for whom he showed not a particle of respect. The disrespect was mutual. Weston's was based on the superiority of birth and the reverence owed to great wealth. He was a young man born with a golden spoon in his mouth. Cromwell had no esteem for the young stud with no social graces except his pride who was unable to keep his pecker in his codpiece and his money in his pocket. Cromwell had done his homework and could quote chapter and verse the status of Francis's financial position. He was so extravagant that he owed his draper, tailor, goldsmith, barber, saddler and shoemaker large sums of money. He was in debt to his embroiderer to the enormous sum of £35 for a gown, coat and doublet cut from cloth of gold. In all, his debts added up to almost a £1,000, a king's ransom that Cromwell was not sure even the Weston's family assets could fully cover. He was, however, impressed by the Weston family's offer to the king of a gift to his treasury of land worth £10,000 in return for a pardon for their son. Cromwell thought to himself that had he been king he would have accepted the bribe, but Henry had said no, a man branded by God as one of the queen's adulterers could not escape God's will; he must die.

The Principal Secretary turned a cold eye on the haughty young gallant standing fearless before him, and said, 'How did you expect to pay off a £1,000 debt; you even accepted £100 from the queen. For what? Services rendered? Or did you think that the king would soon die and Anne Boleyn and her property would belong to you?'

It finally began to dawn on Francis Weston that he was being accused not simply of adultery but having conspired the king's death, and slowly he awoke to the hideous consequence to both his dignity and body. They would mangle and butcher him as if skinning the carcass of a dead stag; they would start with his genitals and move up! He began to tremble and sat suddenly on the stool that Cromwell had provided.

'I do not deserve to die. I have a wife and child. I did not deflower the queen. I swear on Christ's holy cross I am innocent of these terrible charges.'

'That is not what the queen says. She claims you said in public that you came to her chambers because you loved her more than any woman on earth. Who am I to call a liar, the queen or you? I can think of a multitude of reasons for which you should die; you have no sense of the responsibility of money, only its enjoyment; you have been married less than a year but you runt after every women you lay eyes on; you couldn't even find time in your busy fornicating love life to return home for your baby's christening; and you lust after the queen. It makes small difference whether you only thought to copulate with a divinely anointed queen or actually penetrated the forbidden entrance to the satisfaction of your lust. There is nothing further to say. I must leave you to your sorrows and the king's court of law.'

After a badly deflated Weston had left the room, William Brereton was ordered before the Principal Secretary. He was an aging hulk of a man as deadly on the tilting course as he was harsh and cruel in his capacity as a Marcher lord in Wales. The king was overly fond of his uncouth and bullying servant, admiring his ability to unseat his opponent at the joust, allowing him undue influence in his privy chamber and inviting him to witness his marriage to Anne Boleyn. There was nothing supple or agile about Sir William; he could not compete with Weston at bowls or the king at tennis, but what he lacked in finesse he made up for in brute strength and harsh opinions. Cromwell disliked the man, and always thought of him not as a Marcher lord but a warlord, ruling his jurisdiction with a fierce sword and turning the king's law into a personal despotism. He stood for almost everything Cromwell opposed – he followed the feudal rule of the armoured knight flouting the law and doing exactly as he pleased. High on Cromwell's lists of reforms was the introduction of the English system of sheriffs and regally appointed Justices of the Peace in an effort to 'civilize' Wales and bring the king's law to a mountainous area ruled by thieves, cutthroats and armed knights.

Cromwell started the interview by abruptly reminding Brereton of one of his most appalling acts of personal vengeance in defiance of the law. 'You remember the Flintshire gentleman named John ap Eyton?'

'Of course I do.' He stopped in mid-speech, scowled at the Principal Secretary and said, 'I now understand what is happening. This is your revenge!'

'No, Sir William, it is not revenge, it is retribution. You abducted Eyton after he had been accused, tried and acquitted of killing one of your henchmen. You had him strung up by the neck until he strangled to death. If that is your idea of justice, I want no part of it or of you. You regularly brought the king's law into contempt and turned it into an instrument of personal tyranny. The king and all of Wales are well rid of you.'

'Do I get a trial?'

'You will be judged by the rule of law but I can't help it if you are a most unpopular man in the eyes of any London jury.'

Viscount Rochford was the last man on Cromwell's list of potential adulterers. He had saved him to the last because George Boleyn was by far the most difficult but also the most important witness since he was both a nobleman and blatant proof of the queen's misbehaviour. He was the male mirror of his sister, both were devastatingly attractive to the opposite sex, and women swarmed after him like ants to the sugar bowl, both were cruelly witty and articulate, and both were inordinately proud of their own achievements. To meet Lord Rochford for the first time one would take him for a direct descendant of William the Conqueror, so great was his snobbery and self-satisfied delight in his superior good taste and intellectual superiority, when in fact he was as newly elevated to the nobility as Cromwell's great gallery was new to Austin Friars. He was named Viscount Rochford in 1529 when his father was created Earl of Wiltshire and both father and son owed their position to Anne's position at court first as the king's mistress and then as his wife. His French was almost as polished as his sister's; he belonged more openly than she to the reforming gospel, and when not chasing after women, the exception being his wife Jane Parker, he spent his time translating French semi-heretical texts into English and urging the king to allow the Bible to be published in English.

Cromwell came to the point of the interrogation with brutal abruptness: 'You have been sleeping with your sister, my lord. That is in violation of the laws of God and man, an absolute taboo.'

George Boleyn neither trembled nor even looked particularly shocked at the dreadful accusation. He remained the man of refinement that he worked so hard to maintain, and answered the Principal Secretary with a smile. 'You are sure of that?' he queried. 'Given the story of Adam and Eve and the beginning of the human race, incest was a biological necessity that the Church has had to reckon with. I wouldn't call upon God to support your accusation. And who makes such a heinous charge, and what kind of evidence have you manufactured?'

'Your wife, sir. She holds your familiarity with your sister far in excess any normal relationship between siblings.'

'I might have known. Our marriage was conceived in hell and she has hated me and all mankind from the start. You would believe the word of a hateful woman and send a nobleman to his death on such an unsubstantiated charge?'

'The ladies of the queen's chamber have seen you dressed only in your bedclothes entering and leaving the queen's bedchamber. Others have seen you sitting on her bed and heard you laughing and jeering at the king's sexual impotency. You may, Lord Rochford, have been successful in bed with a host of women but they seem to be ready to speak ill of you in their gossip about your character.'

'I refuse to answer your worthless charges, Master Secretary. I see that my words and my silence will be equally used against me. Do not expect me to give evidence against my sister that will lead to her death. I have too much family pride to say a word against her.'

'Yet you have called into question the parentage of the Princess Elizabeth. Isn't that the same as calling your sister a whore?'

'Do your worst, Thomas Cromwell. I will say nothing more on the subject until I am tried and speak my final goodbye.'

'Just remember, my lord, that not even an aristocrat is safe from a traitor's death with its horrible pain and indignity, and must rely on the king's mercy. So mind your words both now and at your trial.'

Cromwell packed up his papers and left the

interrogation room, meeting young Richard at the exit.

'Did you get the confessions you wanted?' Richard asked.

'I did not expect any. Gentlemen do not confess adultery with their queen. But I can say this: the king's privy chamber will be all the better without those four worthless villains.'

George Cavendish was back in town ostensibly to ask Cromwell's advice about a disputed stand of valuable walnut trees claimed by George and his neighbour. More truthfully, Cavendish wanted to attend the queen and her alleged lovers' trials and hoped Cromwell could arrange it. He had been shocked to his soul's core by the adulterous and treasonous actions of his old friend and former charge Mark Smeaton. The two men, along with Cromwell's son, Richard, were sitting enjoying the mid-May weather in the arboretum at Justin Friars. Its owner was particularly proud of two Mediterranean palm trees sent him last year by merchant friends. They had been covered in straw and burlap all winter and now, recently uncovered, Cromwell was inspecting them for buds and evidence of having survived an English winter. 'Splendid,' Cromwell cried out, 'I see signs of growth, eureka! Now, George what did you think of my handling of the common law trials in Westminster Hall this morning?'

'I can't get myself to accept the fact that Mark actually slept with the whore and tried to replace the king's seed with his own. No death can be cruel enough for such an act which was twice abhorrent: he made love to the foulest female in the kingdom, the murderer of the cardinal, and he committed the most abominable treason that a subject can perform, he tried to substitute his common blood for the king's vital fluid. He deserves worse than a traitor's death; his punishment should suit his crime. He should be strung up by his members and left to dangle till they ripped off from the weight of his own body, then left to bleed to death or be disembowelled; I couldn't care less.'

'George, for a peaceful country gentlemen you are excessively bloodthirsty. He was ordered to perform by the queen and threatened with dismissal if he failed to do so. He was also our friend and colleague. I shall try to persuade the king to allow all of them to be mercifully beheaded.'

'Smeaton is the only one to confess his crime. Moreover, he is a commoner. All the others were gentlemen and beheading is proper for them. As well you know, retribution requires that the punishment fit the crime; his testes did the crime and should be severely punished. It is a matter of justice. I can't get over that he allowed himself to sleep with the woman. I thought he hated her almost as much as I do.'

Young Richard injected himself into the conversation when he commented, 'Granted, Smeaton has confessed to adultery, but none of the others have; they insist on their innocence, although without exception they admit to deserving death. That makes no sense.'

'That, my boy, is a coded word among gentleman which Mark did not know; he was brought up, as I was, without decorum or a sense of what is proper to time and place. He made the dreadful mistake of publicly confessing his sins. The others wisely did not. What "deserving death" means is twofold; you may be guilty of the accused but will never admit it or you are guilty of some other heinous crime. In either case, it makes it far more difficult for the government to inflict the awful punishment of hanging, castration and vivisection. It does not guarantee beheading but it makes the ghastly alternate less likely. Admitting that you deserve death for unspecified sins exposes your neck to a quick and merciful death but preserves your balls from emasculation. I wish I could help Mark, he does not deserve what awaits him, but I don't see how I can prevent it. We can only hope that the executioner's blade is sharp and deft and that he cuts off the offending members in a single painless stroke and quickly plunges the knife into the bowels in a place where it will hit a vital organ. Pray he is not ordered to linger and remove each testicle separately, saving the penis to the last.'

'Suite yourself, George, I will still plead for mercy. Next Monday you can wreak vengeance on the queen and her brother who will be tried before a jury of twenty-six peers of the realm presided over by Anne's uncle, the Duke of Norfolk. The trial will take place in the Tower, first the queen's, then Lord Rochford's, whose treason includes incest with his sister. Far more people are demanding entrance for a queen's trial than for the lady's lovers. Benches for 2,000 have been set up.'

'Incest! Disgusting,' proclaimed Cavendish.

Two days later the two men met to discuss and analyse Anne and George Boleyn's condemnation by a unanimous decision of their jury.

Cavendish started the conversation by saying 'I found the most interesting aspects of Anne and her brother's trials were Henry Percy, now Earl of Northumberland and on the jury, collapsing during the evidence of the queen's adultery, and Rochford's public reading of the list of the king's sexual deficiencies. I never liked either man and always thought Percy a weakling and George Boleyn a braggart, but who knows, maybe Northumberland still loved the lady. He certainly supplied a comic moment when he had to be carried into the Tower to recover. Rochford's defiance of your instructions not to read out loud the letter you handed him certainly prejudiced the jury against him but it supplied shocking entertainment of the king's sexual difficulties for every lewd subject to hear. He said, "The king has not the ability to copulate with a woman because he has neither potency nor vigour." He then went even further and called in question whether his sister's daughter was the king's child. I, who detest the woman, could scarcely believe mine own ears at such a suggestion.'

Cromwell was not pleased to have the one moment in the trial that he hoped the king would not hear about pointed out so early in the day. He interrupted his friend before he could go further, and said, 'What made me wonder the most was Anne's insistence on innocence, that she did not deserve death. She alone said that. She denied both adultery and imagining the king's death, and at the conclusion of her performance she spoke her mind in an appallingly brazen fashion. She said, 'My lords, I am clear of all the offences which you laid to my charge. I have ever been a faithful wife to the king, though I do not say I have always shown him that humility which his goodness to me, and the honours to which he raised me, merited. As for my brother and those who are unjustly condemned, I shall lead an endless life with them in peace and joy where I will pray to God for the king and for you my lords.' Those are not words properly spoken by a condemned traitor, and her constant and passionate statements of innocence, even while participating in the mass, bother me.'

'Theatrics,' answered Cavendish, 'she is a consummate actress. Mark would never have falsely pleaded guilty to adultery. Anne is lying through her teeth.'

'I think a more likely explanation is that she achieved a perfect compartmentalisation of her mind, never regarding what she and Mark did as treason. For her it was simply an act of survival, a way of staving off death, and she convinced herself that God would never judge her actions as treason for it was done to save the royal line from extinction, not to destroy it. Her logic was not dissimilar to Sir Thomas More's defence of his treasonous silence; when he discovered the Crown would not grant him legal immunity for anything said in a written justification of his silence, and that he could not speak without endangering his life, he announced that no one had a right to call his refusal to take the oath accepting Anne as queen and Elizabeth as heir stubbornness or treasonous obstinacy. Her action was either that, one of good intentions, or she was lying. Take your choice.'

'I am convinced she lied,' was George's heartfelt conclusion.

'And I,' answered Thomas, 'am not sure.'

Once the queen and her brother were judged Cromwell had gone to the king to sign the death warrants for all six condemned traitors, and he had learned that Henry had already hired a French swordsman for £23 to decapitate the queen. She would not die by the heavy-fisted halberd axe but by the razor-sharp blade of a Gallic broadsword, appropriate, he thought, for a lady who prided herself on her French training and good taste. Norris, Weston, Brereton and Smeaton were scheduled to die on Tower Hill on May the seventeenth. The occasion was public and drew an immense crowd. Smeaton pleaded guilty to adultery;

the others denied both treason and adultery, but they all admitted they deserved death, Weston's last words being 'I had thought to have lived in abomination yet this twenty or thirty years and then to have made amends.' Cromwell wondered exactly what sins warranted the description of abomination.

Mark was the last to step forward to die. By then the block was awash with blood and the headless corpses cast aside in a tangle of arms and legs to get them out of the way for the last beheading. Mark had carefully composed his final words; keep it short, he thought. 'Masters, I pray you to pray for me, for I deserve the death.' He felt himself shudder at the thought of placing his neck on the blood-drenched bloc. Just as this grisly thought entered his mind, he heard horse hoofs beating across the courtyard. A rider galloped up to the deputy governor of the Tower who conducted him to the Duke of Norfolk. In the hush that befell the audience, all three walked up to the scaffold and ordered Mark Smeaton down. Without explanation two guardsmen were told to conduct him back to the Tower. As he entered the fortress he could hear but make out no words of what the duke was explaining to the audience. 'Am I being pardoned?' he asked his guards, unable to comprehend his good luck.

'Don't you wish! Just the opposite, you will be given a full traitor's death the day after the queen and her brother die. No merciful beheading for the likes of a confessed traitor. I will enjoy your screams.'

CHAPTER VII

The Rising Phoenix

Mark Smeaton sat huddled on the damp floor of a dungeon room on the Thames River side of the Tower of London. It was so close to the river that he could sense the water dripping off the stone walls. Anyone trapped down here for a month, he thought, would die of a combination of the flux and consumption. The guards who had deposited him here had said something about a traitor's death administered the day after the queen and her brother were executed. He had tried to judge the passage of time by listening for the commotion of a public execution but guessed the scene would be taking place in the enclosed inner courtyard surrounded by the queen's coronation chambers, the Tower Hall and the Jewel House, which were outside of his hearing, limited as it was by a single barred window some ten feet off the ground and close to the ceiling. There was absolutely no furniture in the room, only grim-looking chains dangling from the walls, a wooden plate, a crockery mug and a pit in one corner for a jakes. It was night and dark as pitch. He couldn't even see the walls surrounding him that felt as if they were silently creeping in to crush him.

The door of his cell suddenly banged open and two figures in the raised torchlight appeared as if by magic. 'Get up and take your clothes off,' a voice commanded. In the flickering light Mark recognised the two guards who had brought him here. 'Do it now.' He did as he was told, and stood before them in his undercloths. 'Everything,' they ordered while congratulating themselves that they had been right in guessing that the prisoner was rich enough to wear undergarments. He did so, and stood stark naked, feeling that it was impossible to feel more helpless and humiliated.

'Why are you stripping me of my clothing?' he weakly asked.

'Because otherwise the executioner would claim them, and since they are remarkably fine for a commoner, we thought we would take them and leave you this.' One of the guards threw Mark a threadbare and loosely woven gown that scarcely covered his nakedness.

'Where are you taking me?'

'Smithfield,' was the blunt reply.

'I thought they burned heretics there. There are no gallows.'

'Silly fellow, you don't think the Principal Secretary to the king would forget something as important in punishing a traitor as the hangman's noose? You are scheduled to get the full treatment; hanging, castration, disembowelment, your body quartered and packed off to the four corners of the kingdom and your head left to rot on a spike on London Bridge. We have been told that the executioner receives a bonus if your heart is still beating when it is torn from your gut. I often wonder about a man's prick; when his members are cut off does it rise to the occasion? I think we will both stay and watch the procedure.'

The horror in store for Mark Smeaton was so ghastly that his legs went numb and he collapsed trembling to the floor.

'Get up you scumbag. We don't want to have to carry you.' The guards came to each side of the prone Mark and lifted him to his feet by grabbing him by the armpits. They then half dragged and half walked him out the door, up steep steps, and out into a courtyard close to the eastern gate of the Tower where a horse and wooden hurdle awaited. They threw him on the sled-like contraption and chained him down, links around his neck, shoulders, waist and ankles. He was thoroughly pinioned. He was glad it was inky dark because his gown had come apart.

Horse and sled got slowly underway with a guard walking on each side holding the beast's bridle; they started down Thames Street headed for Smithfield. The streets were brick and cobblestone and the hurdle clattered and bounced from one brick to the next, turning Mark's brains into a jar full of shaking beans and befuddling all rational thought. 'God this is unbearable,' he half thought, mostly felt. 'I am being shaken apart while still alive.' Unexpectedly, a conscious thought rattled its way into his head. He remembered his first encounter with Anne Boleyn thirteen years before under a beech tree at York Place. She had told him he deserved castration and that should be his fate, and now her prediction was coming true! Mercifully the sled's shaking and rattling made any further dreadful images impossible, and just at the moment he could endure the bumping no longer, the horse stopped, and Mark was unchained and told to stand up. Again he was unable to do so, and was dragged upright to find himself facing a man on horseback. He was still surrounded by hell's darkness but he could discern the circular depression and surrounding stone wall of the Smithfield burning pit with its iron stake to which they bound heretics for incineration. Mark turned away from the awful scene and studied the man on horseback, whom his rattled brains did not recognise.

The rider spoke to the two guards. 'Alright you ruffians, take yourselves off back to the Tower and return the horse and hurdle. I want you both in your beds before dawn. If I hear a whisper of what happened here tonight I will have all four of your ears cut off for slander, and if you blab and speak to anyone I will stretch your neck from here to the Thames River. Here are your wages for tonight. There will be more a year from today if you can keep your tongues from wagging.' He passed down two small bags of coins. 'Now be gone.' They disappeared into the darkness.

'Good morning, Mark,' the mounted figure continued his discourse. 'I thought you might like some company. Don't you recognise me? It is Thomas Cromwell, I have come with the king's mercy.'

Smeaton's response was to burst into tears and cry out, 'For God's sake, Thomas, don't mock me with any more cruelty. You are here to see me die horribly. Couldn't you leave me to die alone in isolation? You of all people know there can be no absolution.'

'You are right, there is no absolution for your sins and I can provide you no pardon, but I have the king's permission to grant you your life on condition that you vanish.'

'I don't understand. I scarcely know my own name! You are really and truly here to save me?'

'Absolutely, I am your saviour, and here is proof: a bundle of freshly laundered clothing. Clothes, they say, make the man; in your case the new man.' Cromwell untied a packet bound to the back of his saddle and tossed it down.

Smeaton looked down at his open gown that concealed nothing, and now the fact he was going to live had registered, he was suddenly overwhelmed with modesty and hurriedly wrapped his skimpy rag around him. 'What magic did you use to persuade the king?'

'Get those clothes on; there is no time to waste. I used no magic; I simply reminded our king that His Majesty could give something more precious than justice for all: mercy for some.' While Mark struggled into his new clothes, Cromwell explained.

'I asked him to recall his Old Testament model for kingship that required not merely a monarch of wrath and vengeance but also a king of mercy and compassion. Majesty without compassion is a travesty. The essence of clemency is its unpredictableness. It is open to all humans, even the most despicable and guilty, but it can never be foreordained. It must be totally capricious as it was in the famous Mantell and Lord Darcy case five years ago. Both men relied on the king's mercy and died; Thomas Cheney, by far the worst culprit of the lot, was pardoned. You may not remember the case; it involved a clash between the old hunting rights of the aristocracy and the sanctity of private property. John Mantell and Thomas Lord Darcy along with Cheney and fourteen henchmen trespassed on Sir Nicholas Pelham's property while hunting deer. His gamekeeper tried to stop them and was killed. Sir Nicholas demanded justice for his dead gamekeeper, and Mantell and Dacry and all his men were arranged in court, found guilty and condemned to death. Despite the pleas on bended knees by the full council that the accidental collective manslaughter by a band of well-bred juvenile delinquents not be punished with death, Henry was adamant and for greater shame both Mantell and Dacry, gentlemen of high degree, were dragged on a hurdle to the place of execution and hanged till dead. The same fate was administered to their cohorts except for four men; Thomas Cheney, who had been in trouble for a similar crime, and three others were all pardoned. Everyone expected the two young and handsome leaders to be reprieved at the last minute but they weren't. No one expected Cheney to get off scot-free but he received the king's mercy. I pointed out to the king that you were in exactly the same position, you had actually confessed to adultery with the queen while the others had all claimed innocence. The king didn't sound as if he had been listening to me, and quite out of the blue asked, "Did Smeaton enjoy fucking her?" I felt that somehow my answer was going to save your life – should it be yes or no and to what degree – and I told him that during your second night with the queen you had penetrated her twice and that clearly implied an ecstatic encounter. The king thought for a moment and then said, "There is at least one bond between the two of us: we both found the harlot rapturous. I can't possibly pardon Smeaton. The Privy Council would never allow it, but, Cromwell, I can do this: save his life. Have him disappear and give him a new life. I never want to hear his name spoken again. I leave the details up to you."'

'Are you actually saying that my having found intense pleasure in having had sex with Anne Boleyn saved my life?'

'That is certainly one way of looking at it.' As Cromwell spoke he began to dismount and untie a bag attached to his saddle. Turning to Mark, he discovered that his friend was having convulsions. Both his hands grasped his crotch as if in protection, his head was bent low, his entire body was jerking with muscular spasms and a gargling noise was sounding from his mouth. Alarmed, Cromwell rushed over to support him, trying to stop the shaking. 'What's wrong, Mark, does the thought of sexually enjoying Anne Boleyn give you a fit?'

Slowly Mark began to get control of himself, stopped convulsing and stood erect. When he spoke his voice was almost a whisper. 'It must be delayed shock and relief. I have been living in unimaginable fear for the last two days thinking about what was in store for me, being turned from a man into a screaming package of pain and degradation. When I stood on the scaffold with my fellow prisoners awaiting execution, I watched each of them die. They died well, without a tremor in their voice, without a sign of fear, and with a smile on their faces. They faced death as gentlemen with dignity and stature. I thought I could do the same, die a gentleman. But then I was hauled off to a horrible dungeon and told I was going to endure a traitor's death with all its ghastly pain and humiliation. I felt sure that I would not be able to endure the pain and would be turned into a beast insane to go on living and screaming to end the agony. Everything I stood for in life would have gone down the drain and I would have known myself for what I was, just another morsel of life pleading for survival. I couldn't bear the thought until just now when it engulfed me in horror. That and the appalling irony that the pleasure I enjoyed in bedding down a queen, whom I really didn't like, saved my life produced a physical reaction that has left me more than a little mad. Did Anne and her brother die equally well?'

'They both left this world magnificently, although George balked at putting his neck down on a block still awash with his sister's blood. Anne herself had it easier. She was first, and probably was unaware when death struck. The swordsman asked her to say her prayer and while she was doing so took out his sword from behind a bale of hay and sliced off her head long before she had finished her Paternoster. Her eyes continued to blink and her lips to shape words even as her head rolled off the block. I wonder what she was saying; probably the words of the Lord's Prayer but you can't be sure. It is strange that we all think that dying well is more important than living well. I guess that's because it give us a chance to make up for all our past failures in life.' Cromwell clapped his friend on the back and said, 'You are beginning to look quite sane to me. You have been through hell and back. No one blames you for succumbing to the shock. Now here is one more gift to you, the last instalment of your New Year's gift. It should keep you going for six months.' He handed Mark a heavy bag of gold and silver coins. 'Now gallop off on my horse and make new history. Here are papers that will make it easier to find passage across the channel to Flanders or France. I have given you a new name; I rather liked the sound of Peter Brueghel, a good Flemish resounding name. I urge you to avoid Dover and find a smaller, less frequented and less popular port of exit.'

'I owe you beyond measure. I am without words, but allow me two final questions: why all the secrecy and the new name, and if I take your horse how are you getting back to Austin Friars?'

'It is part of the king's mercy. He insists that "Mark Smeaton" disappears and that as a historic man you die along with your colleagues in sin on the block. I, as Master of the Rolls, will arrange that; it is merely a matter of shuffling the records. The king felt that there was still vengeance directed at you; some think that even a traitor's death is too kind for the likes of you. They would never forgive the king if they knew you escaped justice but that Norris *et al* didn't. So he insisted that Mark Smeaton die but allowed me to create Peter Brueghel as your new life. As for getting home, I have a spare horse at the Lion's Head inn down the street and around the corner. So don't worry about me. Both Smeatons and Cromwells are survivors. May God bless you, and "good luck" if there really is any such thing. And by the way, I packed your painting equipment and your lyrics and music.'

Mark reached down from his mount, clasped his arms around Cromwell's neck, gave him a massive hug and rode off into the twilight before dawn. As the Principal Secretary walked to the Lion's Head inn he wondered what fate God would allow for Mark. Would he go down in history as one of the many victims of the queen of controversy, would the mythological tale of his terrible punishment for treason become reality, or would the history that Cromwell himself had marked out for him in France and Flanders become the historic truth?

On the way home Cromwell stopped off at the building that housed the Master of the Rolls and made the necessary changes that would prove that Mark Smeaton had died along with the other adulterers. By the time he reached Austin Friars it was only just dawn and he was feeling strangely unwell. He had severe back pains, felt giddy and racked by cold shivers. He wisely elected bed, and that is where Cromwell's servants found him four hours later drenched in a pool of sweat. The sweating sickness usually killed within six hours but Cromwell lingered, barely alive for twenty-four hours, and then crawled out of bed, so weak he could not stand, but still alive. Three days later he was feeling almost well and tried to remember what had happened. He sensed he had gone somewhere that final night before the disease struck but could only remember having been at the Lion's Head tavern for a drink. He must have had far too much to drink, and decided that if anything interesting had happened it would eventually emerge, as bad things so often did.